Hidden

A dark mafia romance

By Lyanna Thomson

Table of Contents

Introduction

I want to thank you you for buying Hidden, a dark mafia romance.

My name is Lyanna Thomson. Ever since I was a little girl I was always fascinated by storytelling and world building. I used to play in my garden, imagining stories and characters, brave knights and princesses, or the evil bad guy who turns out to be good in the end. Now that I am older I've decided to write compelling stories that readers can relate to and have fun reading. I wanted to bring passion and emotion into my stories. Characters that are as brave and mysterious as they are human and relatable. And I believe I did so with Hidden, as you are about to find out. I wish you a lot of fun reading this dark mafia tale!

- From a Declaration of Principles which was accepted and approved equally by a Committee of the American Bar Association and a Committee of

The true mystery of the world is the visible, not the invisible.

-Oscar Wilde

Chapter 1

She trotted slowly. Gently. As if she was afraid that the floor would be hurt if she walked too fast. There were three pieces of luggage rolling behind her. They were piled on top of each other and were all of the same shade of a bright pink colour. As she walked, the biggest luggage which was the one that was below stumbled on a pebble or something of the sort and shook violently. For a minute, it seemed to her as if the luggage would fall over and their contents would spill all over the floor but soon, the luggage steadied and she frowned at them for the umpteenth time that day.

"Pink! What sort of a girl drags matching pink luggage all over in a small British town?" she had asked her mother in exasperation when she had come home with the newly bought luggage. Her mother cracked a childish smile and looked at her with excited blue eyes.

"Why baby... isn't it the colour of every fashionable girl!?" She would be away from her family for over six months.

"I'm not getting any younger, I think I should learn to look after myself!" she had said to her mother when she had initially tried to talk her out about moving out. Her mother had turned on her with flashing eyes.

"Yes... you can assert your independence by leaving home. But halfway around the world is overdoing it. It is taking all of this way out of proportions and I don't think you should do it." Amie had listened and she had argued and she had even joined her mother when she burst into a torrent of tears. But her mind was made up. She was going to have that semester at Colerain and her mother would do herself a lot of good by getting used to the idea. She had packed her bags and had left for the airport on the appointed day, and nearly 72 hours later, here she was. In the streets of the town she had been dreaming for a while now, and on her way to the campus that would house and educate her for the next six to seven months.

Her luggage stumbled again and this time it took a whole lot of fight to finally get it to be steady. She knew that the bags were overfed but she had had no choice. She had sat at the edge of her bed for hours trying to decide which one of her clothes would go and which ones wouldn't. For a girl with humble origins, she definitely had a lot of clothes. It didn't matter, of course, that most of the clothes were cheap or that she bought on sale or on a bargain. She had a lot of them and she loved each and every single one. Eventually, she had decided to just take as much as her bag would take and stop wherever the clothes stopped fitting in the luggage. She still found ways to cramp a whole lot of clothes and shoes in even after it was obvious that the bag could not take anymore. She knew it was silly, but she didn't want to have to shop when she arrived at the new school. She knew she had to watch her spending, especially since she was not sure if there would be accommodation for her on the campus or if she would have to use her meagre savings to rent some shit hole somewhere in town.

"Hey, watch where you're going lassie!" some hunched over man snapped at her as she almost bumped into him. She was lost in her thoughts and seriously finding it hard to keep her mind conscious of her environment.

"Nice! I'm barely here and people are already yelling at me!" she said to herself with a cynical smile. Her phone started to ring and she knew that she could not even dare to fumble with her purse to fetch it. If she let go of the luggage, even for a minute: everything would most likely tumble to the floor and she would look like a total idiot. She paused in her walk anyways and wondered if it really made any sense to pull the luggage all the way to her destination and then back if things didn't work out with the accommodation. She took a quick look around and decided that she knew what to do. Instead of even walking into the school gates that she could see up in front, she would just make a call and find out by phone. If anything, she could feign a sense of importance on the phone and the man... or woman... or fairy... or elf... or gnome might be feeling obliged to let her have a room. She wasn't the sort to resort to this sort of mental blackmail but well... desperate time requires desperate measures. She dragged herself into a tea shop and plopped herself into a seat close to the door as every person in the room turned to look at her. They were obviously puzzled and wondering what might be in her bag. The room was small and the tea lady seemed to have more teeth than anyone Amie had ever seen. She had on a crisply neat dress and a pretty yellow apron over it. She was in what seemed to be her middle ages and had a slight limp. But everyone seemed to be okay with her when she came to Amie's table and asked with a smile that showed her plenty teeth,

"What do you want to have?" Amie made a crisp

order of biscuits and coffee. The woman had looked at her in a weird way and Amie had tried as much as she could not to instantly change her mind and order some tea instead. But she hated tea! She didn't like it one bit and feeling like she was under pressure to drink it made her very uncomfortable. So she looked up at the still smiling woman and said:

"It's okay if you don't have coffee. I'll just have a glass of water with my cookies." And to her chagrin, everyone in the room burst into laughter. Had they all been waiting for her to make a mistake?

"Hey Amanda... you should keep this one. She knows what she wants!" someone called from the crowd and people started laughing again and Amie became scared. What did he mean by she should keep her? Did Amanda eat all the rest who didn't know what they want? Was she some sort of a human trafficker? Amie's heart began to pound in her chest as Amanda bent just a little bit closer towards her and seemed to sniff her. For a second. Then she turned around and yelled on top of her voice.

"Cinnamon cookies and a cup of coffee coming up!" She walked away from Amie and disappeared behind the only other doors in the room apart from the one Amie had come in through.

Amie sat still for a few minutes more before finally concluding that she could relax and wait for her order in peace. Everyone else seemed to have faced their business and she was once again alone. She picked up her purse and rummaged inside it till she found her cell phone. She dialled a number and waited for the recipient of her call to pick up. When a voice came on the other line, her heart skipped a beat.

"Hello.... I am calling in respect of the exchange student's accommodation once again, I just got into town and I was hoping to move in and start my program immediately." She was saying into the phone. The person on the other end was silent till she finished and when she was done, he coughed lightly and proceeded to tell her that there was not long free accommodation for exchange students and that only students that were on scholarship got the accommodation. She would have to find herself a house. By the time he was done, her throat was dry and her hands were tingling. She had thought that she was mentally ready for whatever response she got from the agent, but now as she finally realized that she would have to actually spend her money on accommodation, she panicked inwards. She knew that rent was incredulously expensive in the university town and she would end up using up a huge chunk of her savings. Except she got a job pretty soon, she would be stranded; she closed her eyes in silent prayer and opened it in a flash when she suddenly heard the click of a coffee mug on the table and the clatter of the cookie bowl.

She looked up into the pale brown eyes that stood above her and almost retreated. But for some reason, she stayed and stared back at it. After what seemed like a minute of staring into her eyes, the woman straightened herself and turned away from Amie.

"She isn't scared of me too!"

She exclaimed and a bunch of people who had been watching the show signed their agreement. Amie sat there, wondering what in god’s name was wrong with the weird waitress. She had never been one to go looking for trouble, but she also didn’t back away from them when they get brought to her. The months and months of martial arts training did not leave her empty of ideas of how to protect herself against a bully. She knew she could bring down a man in a matter of minutes and so she usually wasn't afraid of confrontations either with men or women.

She could vividly remember how her interest in martial arts had affected her relationships ever since high school. There was Fred, her first ever boyfriend who wore the green tinted glasses and had his hair in a never changing Mohawk. Now that she looked back at him, she wondered what it was that had attracted her to him in the first place. He had a pale skin. Skin so pale that she ought to have known right away that he was an albino. Then there were those gold irises that made her heart jolt in her chest all the time. She had mistaken that jolt in her chest for love or at least a mad crush. But now that she was older, wiser, she knew better. It was just her very own reaction to the strange look that always seemed to be in his eyes all the time. Besides any of that was the way he dressed! Sweet lord, she still beat herself up over the very thought that she had let him kiss her behind the boys bathroom. How did she manage to fall for a boy like that? She knew that she really ought not to ask that question because deep within her, she knew the answer to it. She had been eager to do what all the other girls were doing. There was Tanya... that black girl that had the longest hair in class. Only heaven knew how she ever managed to grow her hair that long. No matter what all the other girls did, they just never seemed to grow their hair that long. She was the centre of attention of all the boys. That Tanya; she loved them as much as they loved her and she thrived on the attention that they gave her. She walked around school with her extra-long neck and rumour had it that she was dating a college boy who liked to do everything to her in a thousand and one styles. Then there was Beatrice! The one and only Beatrice who walked with her round backside shooting out behind her, seeming to be a detachable part of her body. The gossip on her was that she had had sex so much that she had broken a hip. It was hilarious and a subject for jokes at the beginning but as time wore on, there came to be more jealousy than mockery amongst the girls who gossiped behind her back. All the other girls had been envious of these two reigning queens and wanted to be like them. Amie has never been a girl to be much into the high school spotlight. She got bullied now and then and frequently hated her life. But perhaps it was for the best as it allowed her to focus on her education more and thus excel in most of her subjects. On the downside of it all, she had a terrible social life and lived most of her time in high school as the quiet girl whom people picked on once in awhile.

Then she found martial arts and everything had changed. She started to frequent the kung Fu dojo and soon became pretty known. She lost focus briefly when Tyrell, her albino Mohawk wearing boyfriend came into her life. Then came the one and only party she ever got to attend where he had tried to get all the way. She had stiffly resisted him in spite of the fact that she craved to have the experience so as to be able to talk about something when all the other girls talked about it. On one hand she wanted to be experienced and wanted to enjoy the pleasures that she had gotten hints of when he leaned in to kiss her and when he fumbled around her bra. But that night was different, it was not going to be just a little kissing and fumbling around. It was going to be a journey all the way and somehow, on the other hand, she wasn't sure that she wanted to have that first experience with this Mohawk guy who smelled funny. Forget his golden irises that gave her the jolts, there was nothing much that kept her with him beyond the fact that she wanted to have a boyfriend like all the other girls.

So that night at the party, she had resisted him over and over again and then somehow, he seemed to take the on and off resistance and the seeming uncertainty as his cue that she wanted it and only wanted him to work for it. So he persisted and tried harder. What he didn't know was that he was starting to seem violent and she was starting to be reverted into her self-preserving mode. When she felt that he was starting to be too pushy for her liking, she pushed him away from her a little violently and he came back with just as much force she got really angry and threw a long kick at him which caught him at the jaw just as he started to come back towards her the second time. His lower jaw had slammed against his upper jaw and he had bitten himself through the force of the blow. Before she knew what was happening, she had been covered in his blood and then, perhaps because he had been so scared of the amount of blood, he had fallen down and fainted. She had screamed on top of her voice and ran out of the bathroom cubicle where all of this was happening and into the hallway where there were at least a dozen couples who stood against the doors and walls and seemed to be getting the better of each other. She stumbled her way out of the house where the party was being held and hailed a taxi. It would be a long time before she would even consider the idea of sex all anymore and by that time, she had become old enough to not see the big deal in it anymore and just decided to focus all her attention on all of things that she would rather be doing.

Someone dropped something. She whirled around and saw the mortified face of the defaulter look at the shattered teacup and then at the waitress woman who had now turned around and was glaring at him now. He seemed dazed and lost and she felt a sudden urge to say something nice to him but she turned to her cookies instead and silently dreaded the taste of the coffee. Some part of her somehow assumed that the waitress would have attempted to punish her in some way for choosing coffee over tea. She turned away from the sight of the man with the shattered teacup and concentrated instead on her cookies. She was not going to be drawn into whatever dramatic even that

would most likely be about to happen. She had accommodation arrangements to worry about.
“Are you going to drink the coffee or what? You had me go through all the trouble of getting you coffee and now you look at it as though I poisoned it! “Amie looked up and the woman's eyes were staring down at her again. Something about the woman's eyes reminded her of her albino boyfriend. Maybe something about any pair of eyes that was that close to her face would remind her of the guy. She smiled sheepishly and nodded.
“Certainly! I will drink it...” she said with some hesitation in her voice. The woman looked at her with them eyes again and sighed.
” You have a place to put the luggage?” she talked too fast and Amie didn’t hear her right at first.
“What?”
“I said you got accommodation yet?” Amie’s eyes widened as she realized that the woman was indirectly offering her accommodation.
“No... No... I’m actually worried and don’t know where to start searching for one.” she looked like

she was in deep thought for what seemed like an hour but was really about sixty seconds.

"Well... it so happens that I have a crib that I want to rent out. If you promise to be a good tenant and pay your rent on time in addition of treating the house well, I just might let you stay there for a token." Amie blinked twice. She couldn't believe her luck and if only five minutes before, someone had told her that she would be able to get accommodation there and then and from the waitress lady, she would have laughed it off as a joke.

"Wow! That will be really nice. And of course will pay my rent on time. In fact, I'll pay you for this month up front once I see the place." The waitress exhaled as if she had been holding the breath for a few months and leered over Amie in that intimidating maternal way again.

"Well... finish up with them cookies and drink the coffee. I have an apartment to show you."

Amie nodded obediently and focused on wolfing down the rest of her cookies and calculating in her head how much the fat big breasted waitress would demand for her house.

"I'll bargain. I won't let her cheat me at all." She said to herself as she ate the last of the cookies. But then she looked up into the woman's eyes again and could have sworn that she saw some sort of taunt in her eyes. Something telling her "yea right!!!" as far as her decision not to get cheated was made.

When she was done with the cookies, she gulped down the coffee in two big gulps and realized that that the coffee had actually been well made and tasted nice. She smacked her lips in contentment and felt slightly ashamed of herself for assuming that coffee would be bad by the fact that she was in a town where the majority obviously preferred tea. She stole a glance at the waitress in hopes that she would see something she had not seen before. Something pleasant and even mildly attractive about her. As Far as the few seconds prove was concerned, she didn't see much and she silently and mentally threw in the towel because she didn't know what else to do.

"You done yet?" she turned towards the voice and this time, the woman was not leering at her and definitely not glaring down at her with hungry eyes. She silently thanked her stars and rose out of the chair gently. She slid a few notes onto the table and wondered briefly if she could afford a tip.

"Well... c'mon now!" the woman called with some pinkness coming into her face and Amie put her hand on her luggage and started to drag herself and the luggage after her. For some reason, she was feeling weak and almost like she needed to sleep. She knew however that there was no way she was going to sleep just yet. Maybe when she got to her new apartment... Maybe when she had dumped her luggage in some corner of the room, then and only then would she sleep off and not wake up until the next morning. The large breasted woman led her outside the tea place and then back into a door on the same block. It was a story building that looked old enough to fall. Amie fought the urge to ask the older woman just how old the building was and if it was even safe to live there. There didn't seem to be anything wrong with the building apart from the ancient look that it had and a few statues looking dislocated here and there. Her eyes roamed all over the place skeptically while the older woman looked for what she assumed were keys to the place. After what seemed like an eternity of looking through keys, the door swung open and they both made their entrance.

"I don't always have to use my own keys. There is that good for nothing Dean that lives up there. He gets the door for me. Leave it to me to forget which key opens the main door to a building I own." She said as she promptly launched into a long and detailed history of the place. Amie was not listening. In fact, she had technically zoned out on the rambling of the woman. The only concern on her mind being the general state and look of the house. She could have sworn that the house had not been repainted in all of the whatever centuries it had been standing there. The paints were faded out of recognition and she really couldn't tell what colour

had been on it before. It was a bleached out, faded out version of whatever colour was there at the beginning. There was almost nothing left of it and she could feel the rough surface of the walls as she followed the woman up the dark stairways.
“has anyone actually been living here?” she asked as she pushed a stray spider web away from her eyes wondering how it got there considering the fact the woman had walked ahead of her on the stairs.

“I told you girl... some idiot lives here too!”
Amie frowned slightly and bit her lower lip. She was fast regretting her decision to follow the woman through the house. What if she was being kidnapped? What if she was one of those sociopath women on IDXtra? What if she was going to kill her and eat her liver like Hannibal Lecter? What if she was more like Jack the ripper? What if...
“Here we are!” she declared as she stood at the top of the third flight of stairs and wheezed like an overweight elephant caught in a trap. She looked at her and wondered if she should thank her for taking

the trouble to find her a house or yell her head off at her for bringing her through these ugly and dark hallways. She stepped forward towards the door that she indicated and said a silent prayer that she didn't turn out to be a serial killer and she wasn't about to gut her or cut her throat from ear to ear like those horror movies she had been seeing.

"C'mon... go in. Check it out!"

Amie walked into the room with bated breath. And just as she put one leg into the place, a fat rat scurried over her leg and disappeared behind the long couch that looked like it belonged in some devil's dungeon.

"Oh my God!!!" she screamed as she jumped. It wasn't the fear of rats that made her scream that loud as much as the suddenness of the movement. She jumped backwards and bumped into the large breasted woman that stood behind her. The woman lost her balance and fell backwards. Hitting the floor with a dull thud and Amie falling right on top of her.

The wind was knocked out of both of them and they

remained on top of each other for just a second longer.

"Bloody hell! Trying to kill me, are you, girl?" The woman screamed at the top of her voice. Amie scrambled off her and managed to get to her feet. She then stretched out her hand to the heavy woman in the hopes that she would pull the woman to her feet. The woman took Amie's outstretched hand and started to get up but her weight on the hand was too much and thus again, the both of them fell over each other. This time, Amie took a while to get up and when she eventually did? She was determined not to try and get the woman off the floor anymore. Once she was on her feet, she stood aside and waited for the woman to get off the floor. But she looked at Amie with her haunting eyes and said in an angry voice.

"Hey! Help me up now will you? It's was difficult enough walking up here for your sake... Now all you are doing is standing aside and watching me struggle with the floor!"

Amie nearly burst into laughter as she heard the last

part of the woman's sentence. Indeed, the woman had been struggling with the floor and as she looked at her now, she could see that the woman was distressed. So again, she put out her hand and this time they were able to get her to a standing position. Amie then finally walked into the room with her nerves still on edge from the incident of the rat. As she walked into the place, she looked around the room in dismay. Everything was old and dirty and as she looked through each part of the room.... She became more alarmed and resolute that she would not be paying for the room in this condition. When the short tour of the small one room apartment was done, she turned around and looked the woman in the eyes.

"Thanks for bringing me here and trying to find me an accommodation but I don't think this is the place that I want."

The woman looked her up and down as if she was trying to decide if she was worth the effort of telling her about anything else.

"What is what your budget?" she asked

nonchalantly.

Amie looked up into the ceiling and realized suddenly that the kind of money she was willing to spend on an apartment would determine the sort of apartment she would get.

"I don't know.... somewhere between a hundred to two hundred dollars I guess" she said with a shrug. Thinking in her mind that:

"One hundred dollars plus should surely get me a more presentable apartment than this shit hole!"

She turned to the laughing woman that stood beside her. She was holding her chest as if she was afraid that somehow, it would burst open and the content therein would spill out for all to see.

"Why are you laughing?" She asked her with a slight frown.

"Well... Because you are talking of a hundred to two hundred dollars in a house of three hundred dollars per month. That is nothing short of amazing dear!" the tone was so heavy with sarcasm that Amie suddenly realized that there was no way the woman would be wrong. Houses were expensive in the country that she had chosen to take this semester and she might even have trouble getting a place within that price range. She looked at the woman and shook her head.

"But... but I can't stay here like this! It is so messy and needs a so much repairs!"

"If it's messy, then clean it up. And if it is broken, fix it. That is the problems with you people. You want something cheap with no challenges, but I don't have that here. If you want a beautiful house, you have to be willing and able to pay for it. And if all your money can get you is this place, then you have to wear your fix it cap and take care of things." The woman turned around and started to walk out.

"Hey, so, there is no part of this city where I can get a good accommodation?" she asked the woman as she felt the futility of asking in the first place. The woman would most likely give her the same answers all over again. She sighed and silently wondered what she would do. Somehow, she knew that the older woman was right. She would need a whole lot more than two hundred dollars to get a place that would be what she would have liked. Besides... even if she got a place for three hundred and above, what was the assurance that she would be able to pay the rent at when due? She was already near bankruptcy as it was and choosing to look for a house with that sort of price tag could mean a whole lot of bills for her. She turned around and took a deep breath. She walked over to a window and tried to open it and it promptly came off its hinges. She looked back at the woman who stood by the side of the door with her arms crossed over her voluptuous chest.

"It's not so bad!" she said as she turned around and faced the woman.

"Not so bad. Don't you worry... I'll send Paul up to look through the place and do some fixing!" Amie smiled a little bit now.

"That would be highly appreciated Mrs..."

"Oh... just call me Amanda!" she said with an air. Amie frowned just a little bit and nodded.

"Okay. That would be appreciated Amanda."

"Well then... I'll leave you to unpack!" Again, Amie

was almost pushed to laughter. Unpack? She couldn't possibly unpack in a place like this! She was going to need a minimum of two hours of cleaning work to get the place in an even remotely habitable shape.

"Amanda..." The woman paused at the door while Amie fumbled inside her purse and came up with two neatly folded hundred dollar bills.

"Here... for this month." The woman took the money and looked at Amie with a frown.

"Hey, i know you want three hundred dollars for the place but trust me I can't afford it. The only option is for you to throw me out into the streets right now."

Amanda continued to stare at the girl with a grown and Amie's heart was starting to pound again.

"I should plead with her... I should beg her..."

She was saying within herself.

"Amanda.... Please..."

"Shut up... it's okay. I'll take two hundred and you can pay in instalments." She said a she finally showed all of her teeth and Amie got to see them close up. Amanda did not have more teeth than the average woman, what she really had was a dental malformation that pushed most of her teeth forward and making her frontal teeth seem a whole lot more than it ought to be. She watched the woman get to the door and as a last minute thing said

"Hey Amanda..." The woman looked back and Amie said a barely audible "Thanks"

Amanda frowned again and left. Amie looked around the place and wondered if it was too late to go after Amanda and get her money back. She remained standing on that same point, beside the window for minutes unending after that.

Chapter 2

She collapsed into her new bed and slammed her eyelids shut. She was tired and beat all the way around and was mentally wondering if all the efforts she had put into the place had been worth it. She had scrubbed and mopped and washed and swept. She had dusted and polished and what she had thought would take her about two hours had consumed three whole hours and more from her. It was tiring, she was hungry and ready to drop. At that moment, she couldn't even believe that she had gotten off a twelve hours flight just about five hours earlier. She was yet to get the rest that she sorely needed, and what was worse, the guy that had been sent up to help her with some of the fittings turned out to be more of a burden. She could've swear that she was handier than he was and she had to constantly tell him how to do things.

He nailed the window back in, fixed the bad faucet and oiled the door. He also helped her with tiny bits of this and that but somehow, she felt like he had not done anything that she couldn't have done herself.

She sighed.

This was what she got for flying halfway around the world to study for one semester. What was she thinking exactly? The room looked better ... kind of. But it really didn't matter anymore. She was too tired to be picky and besides... it was a far cry from what it was when she had first walked in. Outside her door was a pile of dead rats that she had killed while the sandy haired handyman plastered himself flat against the wall and looked like he had seen five ghosts and they were coming for him. She hadn't bothered to try to dispose them, she wasn't sure that she would be bothered to anytime soon. "Maybe tomorrow..." She said with a little bit of a satisfied smile. She wanted to display them outside her door perhaps to warn all the other rats against popping their heads into her place. As she lay back in the bed and started to drift off, she made a mental note to call her mother in the morning. Her battery was dead at the moment and the wiring in the house seemed to be faulty. She would get it fixed in the morning. She was happy, having accomplished so much in just one day. She knew that she deserved the rest that she was taking and let herself drift without the tiniest amount of guilt. When she woke up four hours later, the room was in darkness and she was momentarily scared as she tried to figure out where she was. Then her mind cleared little by little and everything seemed to come back into focus.

"Oh... this is that shitty room of mine!"

She thought within herself and smiled in the dark. She was just about to roll over and try to go back to sleep when her eyes caught a tiny ray of light from the wall of the room.

"Light?" she muttered under her breath as she dragged herself out of the bed and towards it. She let her body came in contact with the wall, she traced it out with her hand and covered the hole from which the light was coming. She knew immediately that there was a hole in the wall and she just wasn't sure if what was stuffed with cloth from her side or from the other side. She stuck her little finger into the hole and felt around. She knew instantly that the hole was bigger than that and that it had been stuffed from her side of the wall. Gently, careful not to make any noise that might alert whoever was in the other side, she pulled the small piece of cloth out. It was long and had seemed to have been stuffed in there for quite a while. She placed her eye over the hole so that she could get a better view of what was going on the other side.

On the other side, there was a muscular man without his shirt on. She withdrew from the wall as if she had been bitten by a snake. She rested her back on the wall and looked around as if she was afraid that someone had seen her looking at what she just saw. Her heart thumped a little faster. She pushed her head backwards and closed her eyes for a minute as if to clear her head of whatever it is that had been injected into it by the sight of what she had just seen but it didn't work. She took two big breaths and turned back to the wall and placed her eye over the hole all over again. The sight was the same except for the fact that he was lifting weights, carrying two dumbbells while doing curls. It was a mesmerizing moment for her and she held her breath as she watched him make the movements. His body was slightly wet as he had obviously recently gotten out of the shower. She watched him do his workout. It was obvious that he didn't know that she was there. She was still watching the twitching and the flexing muscles when he suddenly turned around and walked towards the hole and thus towards her. She jerked backwards but not before she was treated to a full view of his amazing six pack that was just in front of her face. She had to constantly remind herself that he didn't even know she was there and couldn't possible have done it intentionally. She kept telling herself that she should just leave the wall and go back to bed, and, maybe in the morning, the nightmare or dream or whatever it was that she was having, would be gone and she would be left with the memories of it. But she knew she couldn't.

As a twenty-three-year-old virgin, she had a whole lot of fantastic thoughts about men and their bodies and what they would be like. She had thought about the weirdest things and the most awkward possibilities but this was the closest she was getting to a weird encounter. She was somewhat afraid but the curiosity and intrigue that she was feeling was way more than the fear and thus she remained plastered to the wall as she watched him moving around the room, trying to put things together and getting ready for bed.

Amie cast a long glance as the wrist watch she had on at the moment and discovered that it was way past two in the morning. Who was this man with the body of an Egyptian God and where had he come from at that time of the night?

What sort of tattoo was that on his back? Who was he and how come she was reacting like this towards him? She wasn't new to seeing male bodies. She had seen a lot on TV and had even watched a lot of movies. None of those things made her feel this way.

She dragged herself back to the bed and slid in. As she drifted back to sleep, she wondered whether the man knew that there was hole in the wall and that he was being watched.

When she woke up and stepped out of her room the next day, the dead rats that she had kept at her door step were all gone. She was a little taken aback and wondered if they had not really died and had scampered away after she had placed them there. She was awake very early that day. As she left her place, the thoughts of the man she had seen on the other side of the wall was on her mind and she was already feeling stressed out at the thought that he would be there every night. She knew that Amanda had mentioned that there was a guy who lived in the other apartment but it had never occurred to her in her wildest dreams that when she finally met this man, it would be a man with a body that looked like it was carved out of stone by the best sculptor in the world. It had never even crossed her mind that he would look handsome talk less of the Greek God quality of handsome that he was. Who was he and what was he doing in a shit hole like the one they shared? The inside of the room had looked well furnished. For example, the Arabian rug that lay at the centre of the room would probably be expensive enough to rent a much better apartment for a whole year. There was no question about it, the content of the room made it obvious that the dweller was not a broke ass person like her. He had enough money to buy that king sized bed that she saw him in and a quilt too. The general decor and appearance of the room told a whole different story from the one that the external appearance of the building told and in fact, a whole new world.

So who was he?

Where did he come from and why did he have that huge dragon tattoo on his back? Was he some sort of assassin like the one she had always seen in movies? Or was he just a bored rich kid who wanted to mess around?

What did it matter?

She was there for her final semester and could barely afford to rent her place. She was going to take a part time job and find a way to pay her bills.

Before she had left the house that morning, she had made sure that she put finishing touches to the place and disposed everything that she didn't want. The place was a clutter but she managed to organize most of it before stepping out the building. She was a neat freak... always wanting everything to be exactly where she left them. This was why she just didn't ever seem to have a roommate throughout college. Then there were the issues of boyfriends. When she had dated Denis... one of her exes, he loved to come over to her house. The awesome part was that he was a neat freak too which meant that he loved to be tidy. The big problem however was that he just couldn't help adjusting something. He always had a different opinion as to where things should be and thus even though they were on the same page as far as being clean was concerned, they constantly had problems on the issues of locations and arrangement. It also definitely did not help that they never seemed to get past second base. Even though he never actually voiced this concern; she knew that it bothered him.

"Maybe I was selfish and unyielding!" she muttered to herself.

"Maybe I should have at least let it happen once" she said...

"Maybe..." she was about to launch into a long serial self-condemning routine, but stopped herself just in time.

“You know what... It doesn’t matter. All of that is gone now.

But she knew that she was already coming to that point where she would have to make a decision about getting laid. The mystery man in the next room was a hunk, but she knew that he most likely would not like her type. Men like him always liked girls with rounded figures and beautiful curves. Not girls who were tall and bland like her. They didn’t like girls who liked books and didn’t fall for stupid pick up lines. They didn’t like girls who did not like to be tossed around like garbage and thus... here she was, alone and in a strange town. Wondering if she would die an old maid or finally get laid at some point.

She went through the rest of her day on the campus trying to get her courses settled and meet her professors one after the other. She knew that it would be a long day and she was ready for it. Handsome hunky men could wait. All she had going for her was her books and she knew that she would be smart not to let it suffer for her fantasy with mister handsome hunk.

When she was done with her business on campus for the day, she grabbed a cab home and rushed straight up the stairs to her apartment. She was eager to have another glimpse of the tall dark and handsome man that she had seen the night before. She wanted to watch him move around, watch him walk, watch him do basically whatever he wanted to do in that room.

She opened her door and went into her room. She rushed out of her clothes, into her pajama, and went straight to the hole. She looked through the hole with her heart going

THUMP THUMP THUMP THUMP and when she tried to steady herself, she only ended up palpitating even worse than she already was. So instead of wasting time on trying to be calm, she looked through the hole and there he was. Seated on a chair and facing the window of his room with his side to her. His hair was loosely hanging around his shoulders and he seemed to be engrossed in whatever he was doing at that desk. On a closer look she noticed that he had a long katana sword in his hands with his palm facing up, his chin kitted out and his eyes looking into the distance with a faraway look in them. In front of him, on the desk was a glass of what seemed like whiskey. He sipped it from time to time and continued to look into the distance. She swallowed and wondered what was wrong with her these days. She had thrown herself into education and research and it was coming to her as a shock to her that she was suddenly reacting like this towards a man that she didn't even know. Yes, he was handsome, but then so were a whole lot of other guys that she had seen before and with whom she had remained neutral. What was it about this mystery man that was so different that she had feel like this towards him? What was special about him? Was it his hair? Or was it the way his torso just seemed to be perfect? Was it the way his abs were so well pronounced and carved? Was it the way his legs stood firm and the way his butt seemed to be barely resting on that chair? Was it because of the way the light of his room caught his eyes the other night or the nearly carved beard that protected his chin from all sorts of things that she didn't even know? She was confused. There was a slight Asian look in his face because of his eyes, but then he seemed like he could be Caribbean or Greek for all she knew. "Maybe he is a mixed race?" she asked herself but then shook her head as of in answer to her own suggestion.

"Well... whatever he is, he is having some tremendous effects on this girl." She thought. Then, in a moment, she heard something clatter to the floor. The sound shattered the peace and tranquillity of whatever he was doing and he rose out of his chair and started to walk towards her again. He seemed disturbed as he walked towards the wall. She sniffed twice in hopes that she would whiff of his scent or perfume or anything at all. But as he came closer... she became scared that he might know that the hole was there. She lunged away from the wall and scrambled away towards her bed. It was getting late and she was ready to turn in for the night but then she wasn't quite ready to let go of the beautiful sight of the glorious Greek God's body. She waited for about ten minutes and then went back to the hole and peeped again.

When she looked through the hole this time, he was sitting at the edge of the bed and looking at something that she couldn't quite make out. She couldn't stop staring at his hands and the strong looking muscles of his biceps. She watched as he turned whatever was in his hand over and over again. She wished he was nearby so that she would be able to carry out all the fantasies that had been going through her mind for the past twenty-four hours. He remained there. Silent and seeming to brood over whatever it was that he was holding in his hands. It was almost becoming painful. She backed away from the wall and decided that staring at him like that was a bad idea. Especially since she knew for sure that he was never going to want her the way she wanted him. She dragged herself into the shower and then into bed.

Chapter 3

Amie walked briskly without really looking up. She wasn't cold. Not really. But she was having a really long day and she was tired and ready to drop. When she had taken the job of a cashier at the grocery store, she had not expected that it would tire her so easily. She had had no idea of how much it would drain her to be constantly on call in a grocery store all the time. She was hungry and ready to bite the next thing that even remotely looked like food in her way.

She remembered how she had walked into the store in response to the "cashier needed" sign she had seen outside. The owner, a shrewd looking man with red face, looked her up and down and asked her why she thought she could be a cashier. It sounded more like she was interviewing for the position of a US senator and she was tempted to walk out of the place and tell him to go eat a ... She shook her head in an attempt to keep the thoughts from her head. She was a very hard-working girl who was willing to work as long as there was someone who was willing to pay. She didn't steal and was an ardent Christian... she also liked animals and enjoyed ministering to the needs of others! Those were the things with which she has answered him instead and he had stared at her incredulously for what seemed like a thousand years when it was really just a little over a minute.

“What? Why don’t you just apply to be a nurse then?” The man had asked her with his mockery evident in his voice. She really didn’t like the way he was behaving but she needed the job because she needed the money. So she remained quiet and waited for him to make up his mind.

“Well... I suppose I could try you for a week and see how you do.” He had said with the tone of a person who was doing her a whole lot of favour. She swallowed hard and tried as much as she could not to grab him and shake him.

“Wow... thank you, sir. When can I start?”

“Right now. Get behind the counter!” he had said and she had been taken aback just a little bit. Then she shrugged. There was no point trying to argue. It wasn’t like she had anything else she would rather be doing. Except of course peeping into the hole in the wall and staring at some strangers firm butt cheeks.

“Okay... When does the night shift come in?”

She asked in a nice voice. He turned around to face her and shook his head.

“No. You are the only cashier I’ll need.” His statement would have been flattering of it done not instantly open her eyes to the fact that she was about to take a job that would use her to the bone and pay her peanuts. She had turned around and faced him instantly.

“I am sorry but I cannot take this job then. You cannot give me a job for at least two people and expect me to be okay with the pay for one.” She said and started to leave. She knew his game. There had been a man in her street back home that used to do the same thing because it would prevent him from hiring permanent staff. She knew the style and she was not going to fall for it.

As she reached the door and started to leave, the man hesitated then said

“Wait...” She had turned around and looked at him with one eyebrow raised as if she didn’t know what he was about to say.
“We don't open all day and all night.” He said. She looked at him askance as if she did not really get what he meant.
“Okay...” She said and made to leave again.
“I’ll pay you for the day time.”
He called after her but she shook her head.
“You either pay me for every hour I’m in here or we don’t have a deal.” She was starting to enjoy the situation. Putting men like this in this sort of position was one that she always wanted to do. Now she was getting her chance and she wasn’t letting it pass her by without doing something about it.
He looked at her with defeat in his eyes and she knew that she had won. Not just for herself, but for every other person that would work for him after her. She had made a difference even though it was small. What she however wasn’t taking into account was the amount of work that would now rest on her shoulders.

As she walked home today, she just wanted to crash into the bed and sleep. She had not really had much time to obsess over the hot man next door. She had left home early every day having signed up for the 6 am classes and was at the store by ten am. The routine had put a lot of strain on her and thus this left her with leaving home early and coming in late. But today was Saturday, and Sunday was her day off. She would soak in a hot bath and stare at the hot man through her secret peephole. It was a well planned arrangement that she had every intention of following.

“I know I might never get a man like that, but there is no rule that says I cannot get off from looking at one.” She said to herself in an effort to quiet the voice in her head that was telling her all about how it was creepy to peep at a man like that. She knew how she would have felt if she was the one who discovered a hole in her wall through which someone had been observing her. She would have been scared and angry and have felt exploited. Maybe she would have even demanded a restraining order. But she knew that men rarely cared much about these things and he would most likely feel more irritated than scared. It didn't really matter to her, she wanted him. But since she couldn't have him, she would make do with watching him from the hole.

Suddenly, she slammed into what seemed to her like a wall. The force was so much that she was thrown backwards and would have fallen right back if he had not stretched out his hand just in time and caught her in place. She looked up into the eyes of the person above her and started into stormy green eyes that seemed to her to be the most haunting pair that she had ever looked into in her entire life.

Her voice ceased.

Her heartbeat tripled in speed

And her knees turned to jelly.

"Oh my god... I'm so sorry... I..." She had entered a full panic mode and started to blab some things that she couldn't even make sense out of. She knew she was repeating the word "sorry" after every other word but she really couldn't be sure of what other things she was saying. He looked down at her but obviously didn't recognise her. He let her arm go gently and muttered something that seemed to her like sorry. She wasn't sure that she heard his voice. Maybe she just watched his lips move and decided that he had said sorry to her. But his face was blank and emotionless. Almost cold. When she came back to her senses, he had walked past her and she was left staring into the distance blankly.

"What was that?" she asked herself. She was confused. He didn't seem to know her, which led her to believe that he had not been peeping back at her. This discovery made her feel even worse for her attitude. She bit her lower lip and continued on home.

"I am gonna have to call in someone to cover that hole permanently..." She said to herself but she knew that she was just saying it and that she would not be doing any such thing. At least not soon.

As she walked towards her building, confused as to what had just happened to her, someone else bumped into her and she knew instantaneously that he had stolen something from her. She looked down and knew without even looking that her purse was gone and when she turned around, the thief was walking away very fast.

“Stop!! Thief!!!” she screamed at the top of her voice. By now however, he broke into a run and she was left with no choice than to run after him.

“Stop!! Please!!! Give me my purse back!!!” she was screaming as the man brushed past more people and ran towards her mystery man. No one paid her any attention. They looked at her and heard her screams. But no one came to her aid. Everyone seemed to be minding their own businesses at that time and she had to do the chasing alone. She picked up the race and sped after the man. There wasn’t any money in the purse. She has learned very early to keep her money either in her socks or shoes whenever she was in an environment that she wasn’t familiar with. But the purse did contain her house keys and a few make up items. Most importantly though, it also held her passport and identity card. The last thing she wanted to have to deal with at that moment was the loss of her identification. What if she needed to go to the embassy for protection? What if she had to get out of town in a hurry? What if...

She ran after the guy with all of her strength. Maybe she wouldn't have even run that much if all what the purse held was money. But at the moment, she ran as if her life depended on it, and indeed her life might have depended on it because there was no way she could be more vulnerable in a strange land except if she didn't have identification.

In spite of her zeal to get the purse back, she could only run and she soon started to grow tired and exhausted. Her breathing became laboured and she slowly dropped off and watched in dismay and distress as the thief appeared like he was getting away.

As he started to run past the tall mystery man, again the man stretched out his hand and caught the runner but this time it was not a gentle catch.

"Hey!" he yelled as he landed a straight punch to the man's jaw that had him sprawled out on the floor in a single swipe of his hand. The moment the thief landed on the floor, he was back up with surprising agility and brought out a pen knife.

"You will wish you didn't do that." he said as he lunged at his attacker. For a minute, Amie's breath ceased as she feared that the thief now had the upper hand as he had a knife. A few people paused in their walk to look in their direction. To them, it was just another brawl between two men who were contesting for the love of the same woman. People who found such fights amusing hung around and the rest moved on as usual.

The thief rushed at him and brandishing the knife dangerously, he said loudly.

"You will pay for hitting me you shit!" Amie's mystery man smiled with one side of his mouth and seemed to brace himself for the attack that was coming unto his person at that moment. But as the thief rushed at him, he grabbed the man's wrist and twisted it out of place in one swift movement. Everyone was left open mouthed as they heard the resounding cracks that signified breaking bones. The mystery man then let go of the screaming thief as his knife clattered to the floor. Amie stood there staring at the man with mouth agape and her eyes popping almost out of their sockets. Perhaps because his adrenaline had been pumped out so much, or perhaps just for show off, the mystery man pulled the thief to his feet and gave him a painful jab before knocking him out flat. As the man crashed to the floor finally, Amie's crush smiled again.

"Poor him!" he muttered under his breath and then picked up the purse from where it had dropped. He handed the purse to a trembling Amie and looking into her eyes with his shocking green eyes, he said "Hold your purse firm. Try not to lose it next time!" she nodded like a puppet and as if on cue, police sirens suddenly filled the air. The crowd dispersed and in the confusion, she discovered that he was gone. She looked around the place for him but he was nowhere to be seen. It was almost as if he had vanished into thin air. As she looked frantically around, she saw the retreating back of a hooded figure. But she could not be sure as to whom it could be. The height and swagger seemed right, but what did she know? She had been too disoriented and shocked to even be sure of anything anymore. She clutched her purse close to her body as if her life depended on it and walked away from the scene. Her heart pounding with adrenaline as if she was the one who had been in a fight. Maybe it had something to do with the fact that she had been running after the thief before her mystery crush came into the picture. Or maybe it had something to do with the fact that she was finding herself to be sorely attracted to the man. This seemed to her to be past the sexuality that he exuded. This was even past his tormenting green eyes. It was something more complex. Less easy to describe in words or song for that matter. She knew she would be unable to detach herself from this man and everything he stood for in her life.

She started to rush through the rest of her journey home. She needed to see him. She wanted to be there when he took his nightly shower and got into bed. She wanted to watch him sleep. She wanted to just watch him. It didn't matter anymore if it was wrong. All of her sense of warning and right and wrong had deserted her and she was left with only her passion. She let it wrap her up.

She took the stairs in twos and threes when she got into the hallway that led to her apartment. Someone else had moved into one of the apartments downstairs and she wondered who else was down on their luck enough to have rented an apartment as horrible as theirs. She rushed her way up the stairs and almost missed her steps once. She made it to the top of the stairs and then to her room relatively safe and sound and rushed into the room. With her heart thumping loudly she went straight to the peep hole and put her eyes over it in the hopes that she would be able to catch him.

Behind the wall was a figure that she instantly knew was different. It was spotless and flawless and had the tattoo of the dragon on her back where he had his exactly. She had long hair black hair that she wore in a ponytail on top of her head. In spite of this, the hair descended well towards her waist. Her hips were broad and her waist was thin. She had the perfect hourglass figure, and a wave of jealousy washed over Aimee.

"I said it!!! He only likes the perfect figure girls!!!" she said as a wave of despair washed over her. In the far corner, he was still seated on his usual chair and looking at the lady with what seemed like a blazing green fire in his eyes. "What would I not give to have him look at me like that!" she thought inside her as she watched the lady walk over to him and sit astride him.

"Oh my baby... I've missed you!" she exclaimed. He didn't seem to be responding at first.

She knew that she had no right to be jealous. The guy didn't even know her. She knew that she had always known that he was bound to have women with beautiful bodies who gave him everything he could have ever wanted. She had always been aware that he would be finding ways to take care of his sexual life one way or another, so why was she mad?

When it was over, she peeped into the wall again and saw her sprawled out in his bed. Amie was angry, but there was nothing she could do about it. Then she heard his voice, it was deep, it was guttural and seemed to come deep within his chest cavity.

"You should leave now." He was not asking. The lady in the bed looked at him with raised eyebrows as if to ask

"Are you kidding?"

"Did you hear me? I need you out of here now." He repeated. She shook her head and turned around to face him.

"But it is already so late in the evening... I could sleep here and leave in the morning."

He rose out of the bed and turned to her fully.

"I don't care. You are a big girl... you can handle a little dark."

"Viper..."

"Don't call me that" She was silent for about three seconds and then turned her chin up defiantly.

"Viper..." She repeated as though she was daring

him.
"You need to come to terms with reality. The Truth is that you are who you are... you will always be."
"Get out!" His voice was hardening. She picked up her clothes and started to dress up. When she was done, she looked at him and blew him a small kiss.
"Ciaos... viper darling. See you soon" she said as she left the room. He looked at the door after her for a while and she watched him sit there and look into space. He seemed to be angry and tormented. His green eyes seemed to have turned to a really dark shade.
He stood from the bed and headed to the chair and table where his whiskey still sat. He poured himself a drink and gulped it down all at once. He looked at the wall for a while, then just when she thought he had calmed down from the anger that was in him, he flung the bottle of whiskey at the wall behind which she was standing. She retreated with bad feeling in her chest. She knew that she would not be getting a good night sleep that night. It was sealed. Questions rolled around and chased each other in

her head. Who was the woman? Why did she have exactly the same tattoo in the same place with him? Why did she call him "Viper"? And why did he seem to hate her? Was that the way he treated the women in his life? Who was he exactly and why was he hiding behind these shabby walls?

Sleep wore its trainers that night and fled. Leaving her restless.

Chapter 4

"Mom you need to stop worrying... I'm not in Afghanistan. I'm in Britain!"

"I know... But I'm not sure what you're going through over there..."

"I'm going through all the usual madness of moving halfway around d the world. What did you expect?"

"I don't know... I miss you"

"I miss you too... so much."

There was silence and Amie knew instantly what was coming. Her mother was very emotional and was definitely the sort of woman to break down and cry on the phone with her daughter. Ever since her father died a few years before, they had been each other's best friends and companion.

"Mom..." Amie called her name. Hoping that by some miracle she would be able to change the topic.

"Hm?" her mother answered

"There's this guy... he..." She was going to launch into the story of how she had moved into the shitty apartment that Amanda rented out to her but realized that she didn't really even know enough about him that would make him worthy of being the topic of a conversation with her mother. She swallowed hard and paused. Knowing that it was too late to back out and she definitely had to give her mother some sort of information no matter what.

"What guy? You met a boy? Oh my God! How cool is that! Something good is coming out of this trip of yours at least!" her mother said everything all in one breath. Amie knew that she had successfully taken her mind off of the loneliness that she was sure she was feeling. The problem, however, was that she had diverted her attention to a topic that was even less discussable than the initial one and she was soon finding herself at crossroads.

"Well... is he handsome?" Amie sighed. The way her mother always became so excited when the talk involved boys amused her. What was it about boys that were so special? She didn't really like discussing the opposite sex with her but now she had no choice.

"Oh well... he's not bad!"

"Well then say yes... Go on a date with him at least but don't kiss him on the first date. And always go with a condom!"

"Mom... stop it! We haven't even talked yet. "

"Well that's not cool. If he's your friend and he wants to be more than that he ought to voice it.

Amie was starting to feel the onslaught of a headache that would prove to be relentless and mighty.

"Mom stop it!! Just stop it."

"If you say so!"

"Thanks... have a good day..."

"Will you be...?" She dropped the call before her mother could complete the sentence.

"Damn! She is just too much!" She said to herself. But she knew that her mother was not doing anything that other mothers wouldn't do. She was cranky for no reason... okay maybe she did have a reason to be cranky but how was she to explain to her mother that in the whole town, she had ended up renting a place like the one she lived in and then discovered a hole in the wall through which she

watched a strange man. Did that even make any sense? She understood that the woman was extraordinarily curvaceous and sexy but so were a whole lot of other women, and he could have picked any one of them. With a body like that, she knew that most women would oblige him without thinking.

Besides... why did they have matching tattoos? Did it have something to do with a friendship pact? Was it like one of those couple twinning things where they got matching tattoos to show their love? If that was the case, then what could have happened to drive them apart enough to make her torture him intentionally and he look at her with that much hate in his eyes?

Or worse still, was the Dragon tattoos a symbol of a cult that they both belonged to? Would it explain why she had said to him: "You cannot run away from me... from your past"? Did it have anything to do with the fact that he was holding that long Asian sword the other day?

Her mind was roaming as she went home. She

wished silently that there was a way she could get answers to the questions that were on her mind. She was curious about him, attracted to him and repulsed by him all at the same time and now she knew that it was only a matter of time before they met again and she would introduce herself to him as his neighbour. She had played and replayed over a hundred scenes in her head about how they would interact if she ever got to meet him again. She drew the bag of bread that she had under her arm closer as she walked into her building and started to tame the stairs in this as she seemed to do every other day now. She was eager to eat something and then resume at her post near the wall. Looking into his apartment and spying on him.

"One would think that I would have some sense and leave the man alone now that I know that he has a woman in his life! But trust me to be as stubborn as a mule!" she said to herself as she turned the key in her apartment lock. She walked into her room and dumped everything in the kitchen at the far end of the room. Then she rushed over to the wall and placed her eyes over her peephole again.

Beyond the wall today was something different. Something she had never seen before. He was alone, on the floor of his room. Fully clothed but obviously bleeding badly. He seemed unconscious and didn't look like he would be coming out of it anytime soon. Her heart started to pound in her chest again. What was she to do? Should she call the police? What if they charged him with something? The fact that he escaped before they came to the scene the other time showed that he either didn't like them much or had a case pending at the station. He seemed like he was not living particularly within the confines of the law and she might be doing him a disservice by calling the cops. She fingered her phone for a while and remembered the times that her father had come home battered and wounded. He was the only other man that she knew who came home bloody and beaten up. He was a fighter.

He never really had a good education and had dropped out of high school to be there for his small family when her mother had gotten pregnant. Then

he had discovered fighting!
He had never been a good fighter... far from it. He didn't even seem like he could fight to save his life. But he went back there, night after night, and got beaten up for money. He would be paired up with some fighter who was still upcoming and training vigorously and he would try to fight the person. Sometimes he would seem like he had a fighting chance but he never really did. Part of his contract was that he would never actually train to fight except his body building. He was there to give a specific set of people some morale and faith in themselves that they could win.
She remembered the nights he would come home battered and looking like steak. Blood shot eyes, broken lips, broken ribs, cuts, swellings and a host of other things that he came home with. He would be tired and bleeding and her mother would shed hot tears as she bandaged him up and stitched him back together. She hated it. And they often argued about it. They would scream at each other and yell their heads off. Then she would burst into tears and

he would spend another thirty minutes to one hour consoling her and promising that he would find a less dangerous job. But he never did and they would have that fight again and again.

He liked the money. He liked that it gave him the opportunity to save for her college education and to give her all the basic things that she ever needed and then just a little bit more. He liked that he could take care of his family with the money he got from his fighting and that was good enough for him. He wasn't ambitious as all of his ambition was vested in his only daughter. She was the only thing in which he had faith. She was all he ever wanted and he did everything he could to make sure that she knew that clearly.

So when one night he had come home again all bloodied up, and her mother had spent hours trying to care for him and crying, they had thought it was just another of those fights and that the sounds were just on the flesh. She had waited for the bleeding to stop after the stitches and it had stopped. Or so she thought. But when he started to lose consciousness, she knew that she had to get him to the hospital. She called in an ambulance and took him to the hospital as fast as they could be. The journey to their house and to the hospital took about thirty minutes and he was pronounced dead on arrival.

He had been bleeding internally.

Amie had been fourteen and had understood that her father was dead. But she had never come to quite get into terms with how he died.

He was her hero... Her super man who got knocked down a thousand times and still came back up. He couldn't be dead! No... It wasn't feasible that he would be dead. He was a strong man who could withstand a lot. So how could he be dead? She had watched people go on the podium and say nice things about her father and she had been momentarily proud. But when it had been her turn, she had stood there and stared into space for a long time. Eventually, she had burst into tears and had been unable to get a single coherent word out to say about her father.

Now as she peeped through the hole and watched the man in the floor, she could feel those emotions coming on so strongly all over again. She could feel herself feeling the pain and the anguish of seeing her father being lowered into the floor. She jerked out of her emotions and rushed out of the room and towards his door. It wasn't until she got to the door before she wondered if it was locked. Deciding to try her luck first, she moved the door knob and the door swung open. She moved closer to him and looked him over.

She pulled his shirt up but realized that trying to take it off him would waste too much time and energy and could also make him even more wounded. She rushed through his kitchen and found a knife with which she tore the short open and the way down. He had multiple stab wounds but not all of them were new. There was a while whole lot of scars on his back, chest, abdomen, and even thighs.

Who was this guy. Why did he have so many stab scars and what kind of life was he living exactly?

She rushed to his mini bar and brought out a bottle of whiskey that she found there. She brought it over to him and smeared some on his wounds to disinfect them and then she rushed back to her own apartment and came back with her knitting kit. Gently and taking care not to injure him more, she started to stitch him up the way her mother had taught her.

It took her over one hour of gentle stitching and bandaging his wounds to get to a level where she would at least be sure that he would not bleed to death. All her fantasies about how she would feel if she got to touch him had flown away and in their place was worry that she might not be doing it right. She almost laughed at the way she had visualized their first physical contact and yet here she was, stitching him up and trying as much as she could not to make a mistake that could kill him. When she was done, the new dilemma became whether to try and move him to the bed or leave him where he was.

He was a big man. Over six feet with all that muscles

and bones. She knew better than to try to move him away from the spot that he was otherwise he might break his stitches open and be worse off than he was when she came in.

“Oh God! Don’t let him die please... don’t let him die!” she said to herself as she packed her personal belongings and started to leave. At the door, she looked back at him and figured that he might be scared when he woke up and noticed that someone had been in his apartment and had stitched him up. She did a double take into the room and found a pen and paper. The she wrote something out on it and then left. Closing the door behind her firmly and wishing there was a way to lock the door without locking him in. What if the person who had stabbed him so badly traced him home and came into his room to find the door unlocked? She decided to be vigilant and look out.

“At the slightest sign of trouble... I’ll call the cops. That’s it.” She said to herself as some sort of assurance of his safety. Once in the privacy of her room, she dragged the only seat in the room close to the wall and peeked in at him. He was still on the same spot but she knew that he would come around eventually and she wanted to see him do so.

"How long are you going to sit here, girl?" she asked herself with a little bit of scorn. But she knew that she dared not leave. If anything happened to him, she would never really forgive herself.

"As long as it takes..." She said as she leaned her head back into the chair and let her mind drift.

In the years after her father's death, she had become overwhelmed with this feeling of lonesomeness that had her looking into space blankly for long stretches of time. Her school work had suffered badly and some of the complaints that her teacher gave was that she was sleeping in class too often. "It is either she is not getting enough sleep at home or she is trying to avoid a reality desperately" the school counsellor, who was a graduate of teen psychology had claimed. Amie had been indifferent as to the diagnosis and had made it to a point to ignore all that was said to her. She was still in awe of how she had made it out of high school. Maybe it had something to do with the time that she discovered that her father had taken out a large life insurance pay on himself to which he made her the sole beneficiary. The only clause being that she didn't get paid except she had graduated college with the college funds that he had left her.

Perhaps it was the money

Perhaps it was the very idea that he had cared so much that he made sure that she was provided for even if he died.

Or maybe it was just the sheer realization that her father cared about her so much that he had practically sold his health and his body to give her a better life. She knew she had to honour it. She had to get the education he wanted and be someone in life. If for nothing else, for the man who had bled to death and suffered spleen rupture for her.

Perhaps this was part of the reason that she had stayed away from the opposite sex for so long. Perhaps a part of her subconscious mind knew that she had to avoid all distractions for as long as she was yet to achieve the things that she wanted to.

Perhaps each time she wiggled away from compromising situations that could lead to her letting down her guard, she was really trying to make sure that there were no stumbling blocks in her path.

Now she was alone

Chapter 5

The room was quiet. Eerily quiet. Outside, there was a heavy breeze blowing and it seemed like the one of those nights when people would need a cuddle after a heavy rain.

Something was not right. The night was stormy. What could be going on to have caused this? There was a banging on one of the walls, maybe a door. She could hear it and she suddenly became afraid. She was scared that perhaps there was a person outside like the one that her cousin Lucy had threatened her with when she was a child. She looked around frantically, looking for a place to escape through but seeing none.

The wind was growing bigger and the building was starting to shake. She could see that there was going to be a disaster if she didn't get out of there in time.

"I have to leave...I have to find a safe place to be. This house is going to collapse in no time and I cannot be here when it happens." Amie was saying to herself over and over again. But then as she circled the room, she noticed that that door was gone and the window was too high up in the wall. She looked around over and over again, trying to find what she had missed but there was no way out. The tower started to shake violently. The room was throwing Amie around and she kept hitting her head against things.

"Oh Lord!!! What is this!!" she screamed over and over again. Then she started to scream.

"Help!!! Help!!!" she was screaming at the top of her voice but it seemed to her that the storm was drowning out her voice. Her heart was pounding and her hands were shaking. She suddenly became cold and that feeling of lonesomeness seemed to cover her up completely. Her heartbeat was at the highest and her eyes were red with the dust that had been raised by the storm. There was that banging again. It was consistent and seemed like the rapping of knuckles on a wall. It suddenly occurred to her that the guy next door would be experiencing the same thing. Was he the one knocking? Was he also trapped in the room? She listened more attentively and was able to make out the sound on her door. It had to be the guy. And there was a door somewhere in the walls.

Screaming and sweating, she woke up with a start.

She looked around wildly and discovered that she was still in her shitty room and there was no storm outside at all. The night was quiet and the breeze was blowing outside the window. She ran a shaking hand through her hair and tried as much as she could to calm herself down. She breathed through her mouth for a few seconds and then looked into the hole to check on him. The room was mostly as she had left it but he was not on the floor anymore. Neither was he on the bed. She could see that the bed was still just as she had left it. She backed out of the chair and slapped herself on the cheek.

“Damn!!! How could I have slept off! How could I have slept off knowing that anything could happen at any time? What do I do now?” she asked herself silently as she rubbed her eyes and yawned. Her mouth was still open in a yawn when the banging came again.

Her heart did a double take as she realized that the banging she had been hearing in her dream had actually been coming from her door. Who could it be that was banging on her door like that? Was it some of the guys who had wounded her neighbour? Did they find out that she tried to help him and have come to kill her? She was shaking and she tried to steady herself as much as possible. A bead of hot sweat rolled down her face and landed on her toes. She shook her head and blinked hard. Somehow, a feeling of déjà vu enveloped her and she started to feel the beginnings of a panic attack. Her mind went through the dream she had been having in the chair near the wall... what sort of stupid dream was that? She wondered. The last time she had had a dream that made her so scared was when she was but a kid. She had had a dream about someone chasing her with a long broom. She had run through the house and into the street and tried to get people to her aid but no one had bothered. It seemed to her that they couldn't even see her. She had run all the way to her mother's office and he'd been told that she had gone home. This meant that she had to run all the way back to the house to find her mother and stop whoever it was that was coming after her with the broom. As she ran back to the house, one minute she would see the person who the broom... the next minute they would be nowhere to be found and just when she thought that she was safe, the person would be back out and the chase would start all over again. She had woken up kicking and screaming and it had taken her mother over ten minutes to convince her that no one was going to come hit her with a broom.

As she walked towards the door, the knock came again and this time it was even louder. Her heart continued to somersault and hands shook even worse than before. The sweat sought to double up and she had to put a hand to her forehead and wipe it off.

"Who is it?" she asked with pounding pulse and hoarse voice. She coughed lightly to clear her voice and asked again.

"Who is it?"

There was no response and she panicked.

"Oh my god! Maybe they are here to kill me!' she could feel her veins contracting from the pressure of the blood pumping through her.

She walked over to the door and looked outside through the peephole and there he was. Her heart slammed in her chest and then seemed to have stopped beating altogether. Now she really couldn't tell which would be worse. Being killed at that moment by a bunch of bloodthirsty katana wielding murderers or to have to face him. She hesitated and looked at herself briefly in the mirror at the other side of the room before she pulled the door open with as much of a smile as she could muster at the moment.

“Hello...” She said with a face that was as innocent as she could make it.

“Hello” he said with a slight bow. She almost bowed back. But she didn't. She was freaking out in her mind.

“What does he want? What does he want me to do? Does he know that i’m the one who was in his room? Is he mad at me? Is he here to kill me? She was practically shaking from head to toe as she held onto the door frame as if her life depended on it. And perhaps it did depend on it as she tried as much as she could not to look into his eyes.

“You’re Amie.” It wasn’t a question. It was obvious that he knew her. There seemed to be more knowledge in his eyes about her than what she knew of him. How long had he known her? How much did he know of her? Was he aware that she had been peeping at him through the hole? Did he know that she had seen his lady friend from the other day? She bit her lower lip and tried not to blurt out all of the questions that were on her mind at that time.

“Were you the one that came into my apartment?” This was obviously a question but it didn’t really sound like one. It sounded more like one of those times when her mother asked her if she was the one who stole the cookie and even though she knew the answer to the question. Amie looked at her fingers, then to his face and then to something that was behind the door.

“That... “She started to say but she paused.

“That right there is a good question and the answer to it is no. I did not... come into your apartment” if she had been listening to herself, she would have recognised the lies in her voice in that moment.

“I’m sorry” She said and then instantly hung her head in shame as she watched the amused smile that was on his face. He knew... and he was mad at her for lying. She closed her eyes briefly and silently prayed that the earth would open up and just take her away from him at that moment.

“Well... I was just about to go have some tea and I

wondered if you might want to share with me seeing as we haven't got a chance to be properly acquainted since we became neighbours. That is if you don't mind of course" he said with the amused look on his face again. She almost yelled "no" and run back into the apartment. But she sheepishly nodded a yes instead and when he turned around, she proceeded with

"I take coffee..." She mumbled with a small smile. He nodded

"I know... coffee then?" he asked with one eyebrow raised. It was obvious to her that he was laughing at her.

"Yes..."

"Okay... Do you want to change out of that?" he nodded at her outfit of an old t shirt and a pair of bum shorts. Her hair was somewhat tousled and her face was bright pink from all the excitement in her body system. She nodded briefly and turned around and closed the door. Actually, she slammed the door because she was too jittery. She rushed through her bunch of clothes and pulled on a shirt but left her shorts on. Then she ran a brush through her hair and rushed out.

"Ready?" he asked with some sort of look that had her wanting to rush back in and check herself out in the mirror just to be sure.

"It's too late for that now" she said to herself and shrugged mentally.

"Yes..." She said instead and he smiled broadly. Showing a beautiful sparkling white set of teeth. Her nerves were calming down now and she was starting to be less panicked. She was stealing looks at him and was doing all she could not to seem like a love struck teenager. She was silently glad that he seemed to be okay in spite of the wounds that he had sustained. It wasn't like any of them were immediately life threatening, but if the wounds had been left untreated, they would have gotten infected and that could then become life threatening. He seemed okay... all things considered and she was silently glad. This could as well be some Hollywood movie for her. She being the secret doctor or nurse who fixed people up without them knowing. Presently, she looked at him as he turned around.

"Good... Come with me" He said. She hesitated briefly, wondering if it was too late to say no to the whole tea coffee idea. What if she said something he didn't like? "What if she..." she shook her head again as if to shake the thoughts out of it. Then, seeing him walking down towards the descending stairs, she shrugged and then she followed him with her heart pounding in her ears. She made efforts not to step on his feet as she walked behind him. It was obvious to her that if her heart continued to pound like that, she might just faint and get it over with. Perhaps then he would have to be the one looking after her.

Chapter 6

He walked in front of her down into the street. He wasn't in a hurry, letting his long legs just move over the floor like he owned all the time in the world. Amie could notice this because she was one to walk in a directly opposite manner. She was always in a hurry and liked to get everything done as soon as she could. She was not one to have the luxury of slowing down to savour anything. She studied hard and fast and even when all she was doing is cleaning, she liked to do it on a time frame. She didn't like that he was walking so slowly but there was nothing much she could do. She was too shy to complain, and then to make matters worse, as they burst out into the busy evening streets, he took her hand in his. Thus, making it impossible for her to go at a different pace from him.

"So what are you doing in this town?" she asked. He shook his head and said in a voice that only she could hear.

"No talking on the road... we will talk, but not here!" she was confused. What is with this guy? No talking on the road? What was going to happen? Would the birds of the sky listen to him and tell everyone whatever he is talking about at that moment? She sighed frustrated. First he was walking like a snail and now he didn't want to talk. She shrugged her mental shoulders and decided to just let things be.

"If I ever go out with him again, I will give him conditions." She said to herself just as he took her around a corner and then bringing her to stand in front of him, he put both of his hands on her shoulders and walked her into the house. It was a somewhat childish gesture and she laughed lightly. They walked to a table that sat alone in a far off corner and sat at it.

"Coffee please!" he called and she looked at him and smiled. He knew what she took...

"So tell me about you. Why do I get the feeling that you are hiding from something?" she asked him with a serious look on her face.

"Maybe because I am." He answered with a mischievous smile. She smiled and nodded as if she understood. She wasn't going to be one of those Hollywood girls who would freak out.

"What are you hiding from?" she asked with an air of secrecy. Again, he laughed a little bit. The way she looked at him as she leaned towards him with her face animated with the joy of being told a secret just made him want to laugh hard.

“Well... let me see...” he started and her face could not have betrayed her more. She was excited to hear a secret. His secret. She leaned towards him with anticipation written all over her face and nodded when he paused

“Go on... don’t be afraid!” she cooed and he giggled.

“In my hometown far away in Asia...”

“... Yes?” she nodded again like the little gossip girl that she was.

“There is this king...”

“...okay” she said again. She could not help it, she was cutting into his sentences.

“Well, he hates me and wants me dead...” she nodded again. It made perfect sense to her and he pulled on his most serious face and said to her.

“Now the king has a giant monster mushroom that he sends to people to deal with them whenever he doesn't like them. The giant monster mushroom is coming after me now” she frowned. What sort of a story was this? This was not some sort of fairy tale, this was reality. How did a giant mushroom fit into the picture? She looked at him with one eyebrow raised.

"Oh... giant monster mushroom is the name of a man?" he shook his head with amusement on his face.

"Nope... it is the name of a mushroom. You know... an actual mushroom!" she was starting to get frustrated as it suddenly started to occur to her that he had been pulling her legs all the while. There was no king and definitely no mushroom. She could have cried with the anger of her frustration at that moment.

"Are you kidding me right now? You have been telling me a fable all this while?" he couldn't hold back anymore, he burst into a fit of laughter and he must have popped one of his stitches because he groaned painfully and she soon saw a darkening under his black shirt.

"Shit! You popped your stitches?" she asked. She was instantly back to her caring mode but then she had just given herself away as the person who actually went into his room and stitched him up.

“How did you know that I have stitches if you didn’t put it there?” he asked with a slight frown. Her heart slammed in her chest as she realized that she had made a booboo and could not lie about her involvement in his stitches anymore.

“Oh crap! Now he will never trust me again!” she said to herself. She was feeling quite sad about the whole affair and could have run away if the door wasn’t so far away. She dropped her head in shame and he stretched his hand and touched hers.

“Hey... I'm not mad... I think what you did for me was heroic. You saved my life...

“Well... your wounds were not really life threatening.” She said and he shook his head with a small smile.

“You know very well how wrong that statement is. You disinfected my wounds with alcohol and sugar and stitched me up. If you didn’t do that, I would most likely have gotten infected and then what?”

She nodded in a small way and looked away from

him. She didn't know why but a wave of grief suddenly washed over her as she remembered the father she lost and how she wished that he was still in her life. He must have sensed her grief because his hand covered hers completely and his thumb caressed her.

"Hey... It is okay... but today is not the day to grief. Today is a coffee and tea drinking day. She smiled at his joke. He was right. It was hardly the time to be sad and tearful. Indeed, it was a day to drink coffee and talk to a tall handsome Asian stranger who had come home earlier that day with life threatening wounds. Life was so full of such ironies. Before she could say anything in answer to the things that he had said, the waitress appeared with their orders.

"Hey I didn't order muffins!" she said with a slight frown when she was served.

"I always order some muffins with my tea, so she figured you might want some with your coffee too."

"Oh..." was her response as she picked up the muffins and dug into it with relish.

"Hmmmm... it is delicious... so good!" she exclaimed with a mouthful of muffins and crumbs sitting all around her mouth. He was looking at her mouth with a long look on his face and she actually leaned back from him a little.

"Hey... what you staring at me like that for?" she asked with a raised eyebrow.

"I don't know... you eat like a child." He said simply as he raised his tea to his mouth gently. She had managed to finish her muffins and was looking longingly at the round muff that sat in his tray.

"Don't even think about it! I'll kick you so hard you will need an oxygen tank to get back the air I knocked out of you." He said and she flinched slightly.

"Hey... come back here. You can have the damn muffins and don't give me that look. You're the one robbing, me of my muffins so cheer up and eat. Lil miss grubby!" he exclaimed.

"How come you talk with so little accent?" she asked with wonder in her eyes as it was her turn to stare at his lips as he talked.

"I don't know. Maybe because I was originally born in the United States and I lived there till I was twelve!"

"Ohhhh... so you are United States citizen?"

"I think I am. Do you think I am?" he asked with a comically clueless look on his face.

"I think you are!" she said with mirth.

"Come..." he said standing up and pulling her with him.

"Let's get out of here." She let him pull her out of her chair and let him drag her across the room.

"Aren't you going to pay them?" she asked as they neared the door. Again, he smiled and looked at her "Why... I already paid her" it was a riddle that she wished she could solve. She watched him wave goodbye to the woman behind the counter and she watched her wave him back with a full smile. When did he pay her? How did her pay her? Because as far as she had seen, as far as she could see, he had not paid her at all but had just come into the place and ate her muffins and drank her tea for free. She wanted to question him but the crowd in the streets

were deafening so she didn't bother. At least not yet.
"Where are we going?" she asked him as loud as she could when she noticed that he wasn't leading her towards their house.
"To deliver you to the giant mushroom instead of me!" he said with mischief again. The corners of his eyes were crinkling and the excitement in his voice was palpable even over all the noise of the multitudes in the streets.
She laughed. It was a loud feisty laughter and he loved it,
"But for real... where are we going to?" he shook his head.
"It's a surprise. Tell me you like surprises." She smiled. She wanted to tell him:
"Yes I like surprises if it is tall and handsome, with beautiful lips." But she didn't. Instead, she just nodded and decided to wait and see what the tall dark and handsome surprise had for her as a surprise of his own.
"Okay." he said as he took hold of her hand and started to manoeuvre her round the crowd. She

noticed that the crowd seemed to be moving in the same directions. They all wore colourful clothing and she could already see some fireworks going off in the distance.

“Does your giant mushroom monster by any means have anything to do with fireworks and colourful clothes?” she asked with a smile as she suddenly started to realize that it was a carnival going on. He shrugged as if he had no idea and then before she could press him for an answer, a loudspeaker somewhere began to blare some really nice music she looked around her and suddenly, it seemed like she had been surrounded by all these dancing people. She would never have guessed that the town had a population that huge and as she watched them, she started to feel excited.

“For tonight's is gonna be a good night...

For tonight is gonna be a good good night!” the speaker was saying and she was nodding.

“Dance if you want to, silly, and stop nodding your head!” he yelled over the din of the music.

“I'm a horrible dancer!” she screamed back.

"Well then... let's step on each other's toes all night long. I am worse than horrible." She laughed as she tried to imagine him dancing all over the place. She knew that it would be some sight and she would have given a lot for the opportunity to see that.

"How is your stitch? Is it still bleeding?" she screamed at him. He shook his head and frowned.

"Why are you yelling?" he asked her and she realized for the first time that each time she talked to him since they had been in the crowd, she had been yelling but each time he talked to her, he had only moved his lips and yet she had been able to tell what he was saying. It was a sudden realization as she realized that she could read lips.

"Oh my god! Are you kidding?" she whispered to him and he smiled. Finally, she got it. They didn't need to scream to hear each other over all the noise. They could hear each other without their voices.

"Come here!" she pulled him into a warm embrace. It was her way of saying thank you to him for having shown her that she could communicate without voices.

"Come... let's get out of here and take a walk." He said to her

"But we haven't danced yet." She grumbled.

"Okay... twenty minutes of dance." He said with a look of authority.

"Thirty" she countered with her defiance obvious on her face and body. And he shook his head.

"Twenty-five." He said with a note of finality in his face.

"Deal!" they shook hands and she immediately launched into all sorts of body gyrations that had nothing to do with coherent dancing. She was all over the place and actually stepping on his toes like he had predicted that she would.

"Hey., you are going to need to calm down with all that shaking okay?"

He said and she laughed in his face and continued her dance. He watched her with amused tolerance. She was moving around like a drunk penguin and he made a mental note to tell her just that the first chance he got.

She started to back her backside into him with

seductive movements that made him open his eyes wide and the go straight faced instantly. He could feel himself responding to every movement she made, either she touched him or not. She had a way of capturing his attention and holding it while she danced like a maniac all over the place. She was sweating as her body bent into unbelievable angles and her waist gyrated in the spasm of excitement. He watched her warily at first, wondering how she could claim not to know how to dance but know to wiggle her thin waist like that.

"If she knew how to dance, I would be dead!" he said to himself sarcastically. The music was growing faster and her body was responding to it. Moving to the beat so synchronously that he started to wonder as to which one of the two was following who. Was the music following her or was she following the music?

The music rounded up with a series of drumbeats and came to a stop abruptly and if he didn't know better, he would have thought that she had practiced and rehearsed her own ending as well. The minute she was done, he lifted her into the air in appreciation of all the dancing and she screamed. Her legs flailed about in the air as he swirled around with her in his arms. People moved backwards and away from them in order to give them space.

"Put me down... put me down this instant" she was screaming and he laughed at her. After a few minutes of her blushing furiously and asking him to put her down, he finally relented and placed her on her feet gently. The minute her feet were on the ground, she felt a spell of dizziness wash over her and he had to grab her to prevent her from falling. He held her that way for a while until she was finally able to stand by herself.

"Can we go now?" he asked when she was done and she nodded breathlessly as beads of sweat poured from her face unto her neck and chest.

"Come." He said simply and took her hand. Again, he led her through the crowd of people and they walked westward when they burst out into the empty street.

The night away from the carnival ground was quiet and full of the voices of chirping birds. As they walked away from the carnival ground, she looked back and saw the lights in the distance. Something about the way the lights glowed in the distance got to her and she smiled quietly. Talk of romance finding unromantic people.

He walked her towards a small twenty-four-hour park and putting his hands on her shoulder; he made her seat and then sat next to her. After a few moments of silence, he said to her almost quietly.

"So... tell me about you." She looked down at her hand and shook her head. What was there to tell? What was she to tell him? That she was a book nerd who just liked to peep at some guy through the hole in the wall between their rooms? That she was an only child and that she had left her mother to come far away for learning because a part of her was scared that something would happen to her? That she was a Christian who only went to church when she remembered and only prayed when she needed help? There were so many things she could tell him

about herself but none of them was flattering enough information so she kept her mouth shut for the moment and instead smiled like a cornered cow.
"What is funny?" he asked her with his solemn voice.
"Nothing... what would you like to know about me?" she said to him. He hesitated slightly. Then he scratched his hairy head as if he was trying to remember something.
"Well... tell me about your family back home." He had somehow gotten himself to the one topic she wasn't sure she wanted to discuss. The minute he mentioned "family", she knew that the night was about to become emotional for her.
"Well... my dad is dead. I used to live with my mom until I went to college and then came over here." She said simply. She hoped that the shortness of her sentence would tell him to back off. He looked at her for a minute and then started to fish for something in the folds of his jacket.
"Do you like popsicles?" he asked offhandedly.
"I guess... they're not too bad." She said. Wondering

what the hell popsicles had to do with what they had just started to talk about.

"Here." He said as he handed her one rather large one. She unwrapped it and promptly popped it into her mouth. He was still looking at her and this time, she was starting to feel really uncomfortable with the way his eyes seemed to bore holes into every inch of her body. Why was he staring at her like that? Was he hoping to see through her soul and gather all the information that she was not volunteering? Or was he just intentionally trying to rile her in the hopes that somehow, she would eventually break down and confess everything about her family? What sort of game was he playing and what was his aim? She looked away from him and pretended like she couldn't care less if he was looking at her in that weird way. After what seemed like year of trying to seem indifferent, she gave up the battle and looked at his face.

"Why are you looking at me like that?" she blurted.

He smiled at her question and then shook his head.

"Well, let me ask you this. Do you trust me?" she

looked at him and wanted to laugh. What the hell did he mean did she trust him? Of course not. At least not really. He was practically a stranger and come to think of it, she didn't even know his name. She had known not to trust that waitress' words after she sent that poor excuse for anything as a handyman to help her fix her place up. She had mentioned that her next door neighbour would be a man named "Dean" but this man looked many things but Dean. In spite of the fact that his accent was little and was not really interfering with his English, the dragon tattoo on his back and the katana in his room were enough evidences that he was a man that was very in touch with his Japanese roots and was very unlikely to have a western name like Dean. She didn't know him. She couldn't possibly trust him. But how was she to tell him this without making him feel bad and putting him off for good? How was she to remain his friend if she ended up pissing him off by saying that she didn't trust him? She swallowed hard and looked at him with hopes that her eyes showed some sincerity.

"Well... we don't really know each other that much... and you could be anyone for all I know, I am not afraid that you might do me harm because I don't think that you have a motive to, but at the same time, I can't really say that I trust you." He nodded as if he understood everything she had just said.

"Yet you unwrapped that Popsicle and plopped it in your mouth almost immediately. What makes you sure that what you have in your mouth at this minute is not laced with poison?" her eyes opened wider and she pulled the sweet out of her mouth in response to what he had just said.

"Oh my God! Why would you poison me?" she asked with wide eyes as she looked at the Popsicle with wide fearful eyes. He shook his head. "That is the wrong question right now." He said and she listened. Waiting for her body to show signs that she had been poisoned.

"*What have I gotten myself into? I knew there was more to this guy right from the beginning. I just didn't know that he could want to kill me just for the fun of it!"* she was thinking to herself.

"The right question right now is why did you trust me with your life and body? You don't even know my name, yet I offered you something and you not only took it but stuck it in your mouth immediately without scrutiny. Tell me, what is the colour of the popsicle in your hand? Don't look at it!" he said and she was starting to realize that he was right. She really didn't know the colour of the popsicle she had in her hand. Hell she didn't even know the maker!

"I... I'm not sure. Red?"

"Purple. It is purple." He said and then she looked at it and saw that he was right. The colour of the popsicle was purple. She shook her head at herself gently for her behaviour.

"so let me guess, you already trusted me with your safety, you have trusted me with your life, but you will not trust me with an information that really would be of no use to me but an avenue to get to know you?" she suddenly realized what angle he was coming from. Taking the popsicle from him and eating it without even bothering to check what it really was or what colour it was showed some amount of trust that ought to be extended to telling each other about themselves. He was right, in not wanting to talk to him about her family, she had been irrational. Considering the fact that she would take something from him and eat it without bothering to investigate what it was.

“I'm sorry.” She said with her face averted.

“There is nothing to be sorry about. I just wanted you to see that you already subconsciously trust me. You just have to let your conscious mind do it too.”

She nodded. Still wondering if the popsicle was poisoned. As if he could read her mind, he giggled and shook his head again.

“And no... I did not poison the popsicle. You are not going to die” she burst out laughing then and let her head rest on his shoulder with a slight bounce. They were both quiet and looking at the sky as though there was something interesting about it.

“My dad... he was a wrestler. No... He was a street fighter. Not really a wrestler.” She paused as if she was getting memories that she really would rather not have.

“He used to be in the beginning of the fights. One of the first rounds. He would get beaten up most times as part of his job was to get beaten up. He was being paid to lose...”

The night was still and her voice seemed to be floating on the surface and into the distant places. Somehow, when he noticed that she had started to tell him the story about herself, she put his arm around her shoulder just so she would feel secure and trust him all the way.

“... He would come back home bruised and wounded. Lose a lot of blood and often spend weeks recovering. My mother would stitch him up and tend his wounds. She is a nurse, but she ended up nursing him more than any other patient she ever had. Sometimes, I would come back from school to find him in his bed, unconscious and her by his side, sitting and waiting in agony for the moment when he would come to his senses. There wasn’t enough money for much of a health insurance and thus, she had to treat him as much as she could by herself.

She only had him go to see a doctor when she knew that she could not handle him alone. Then one day, she could not handle him at all..."

Amie's eyes were looking into the distance. Seeming to see everything and nothing at the same time. He sat there and watched her as she told him the story that brought lumps to her chest and tears to her eyes. How her mother had knelt in front of her and had told her while holding her hands that her father was dead. How she had stared at her in disbelief and shock and had remained in that exact state right up to the moment that he was buried two weeks later. How she had suddenly realized that the funeral was indeed the one last time she would get to see her father and how that had set her up for the nightmares that came over and over again for the next one year. She hadn't found the right amount of tears to mourn him, but she had felt that vacuum, that emptiness every day since that day that she had said goodbye to him.

He sat there and watched her talk. His hand remained on her shoulder and as her mouth moved with her words, her throat vibrated against his shoulders. Sending silent shivers down his spine. He kept his arm around her as if to dare anyone or anything to touch her ever again. When she was done, his fingers squeezed her shoulder gently over and over again. He waited for over twenty minutes for her to be composed before he said anything. When he was sure that she was calm enough and that the silent tears had ceased and her voice was clear, he said to her in a gentle voice

"If this counts, you seem to me like a very energetic and positive person, you have not allowed the pain of your past to influence your life too much..." he said. And, when she looked up at him as if she was about to disagree, he quickly added

"Except for the fact that you ran away from home and all the memories of happiness with him reminded you again of how it was back in the past. She smiled. That was exactly what had been on her mind. She nodded.

"Except for that." They were silent again for some minutes before she gathered her wits about her and pulled away from him for a bit.

“When you said that the popsicle was poisoned, you sounded so real. I actually believed you. Is this something that you could do?” his eyes hardened for just a second and she would not have seen it if she had not been looking into his eyes when she asked her question. He looked away from her for fear that she might find the truth in his eyes. He cleared his throat as if he was trying to decide what best to tell her.

“To be honest with you, Amie, I am not a saint. In fact, I am very far from that word. In reality, I am closer to the opposite of the word than the word. I have done a lot of bad things in my life and one of the reasons I am here is because I am trying to get away from all that and start all over.” She blinked twice, trying to figure out what part of all he had just told her he had actually confessed to killing someone before. What did he mean by “bad things”? Just how far had he gone? Fraud? Blackmail? Murder? What exactly would be the accurate description of the nature of his crime? She sat there and looked into the distance until he said with a heavy voice.

“I think we should get moving.”

She nodded without a word and stood with him.

“My legs are weak.” She said gently.

“I’ll carry you.” He said and before she could protest, he lifted her onto his back and started the long walk towards their streets which was several blocks away.

“By the way, my name is Shin... if you have joined the group of people who call me “Dean” I'll kick you when I hear you say that.” She laughed heartily and let him carry her for nearly three blocks before starting to fight for her freedom again.

He eventually dropped her and held her hand while they ascended the stairs quietly. Each ruminating about these last few minutes that would be so crucial in their friendship henceforth. When they walked past his door and he did not stop or invite her into the place, her head instantly started to calculate as to if her apartment was in the best of shapes. She started to think within her as to if the place was going to impress him or put him off. She didn't really have much to worry about; she was a neat freak and always kept her home tidy, what she didn't know, however, is if the place was going to be to taste in terms of furnishing or if he would turn his nose up at it.

At her door, she paused and started to fumble with the keys.

When he said "goodnight" her heart leapt violently as she suddenly realized that he had no intentions of coming in with her to consummate this newly found friendship of theirs. She looked into his eyes, searching for clues of what to do to get what she so desperately wanted but there was nothing in them. At least nothing that she could really decipher. Reluctantly, she returned his "goodnight" and opened her door. Once she was inside, she heard his footsteps going down the hall. It didn't break even once. Her heart sank into the night until she fell asleep.

Chapter 7

The wall clock in the far end of the store chimed and Amie looked up in glee. If the world was filled with people full of happiness, she would be the happiest of them all. In the last few weeks since she became acquainted with him, she had been exceptionally happy with the turnout of events. It seemed to her that she was spending most of her free time thinking about him now.

From the day of the carnival, he had seemed aloof again. Leaving before she was awake and coming back to the apartment after she had slept. It was starting to seem to her like he was avoiding her but she couldn't be sure. She often tried to stay awake long enough to catch him come into the house but she never seemed to be able to do it. It was as if he could see her and would wait for her to be asleep before he came back into his apartment.
The events of the night of the carnival played on in her mind from time to time. The way he had looked

into her eyes and listened to her as if his life depended on it. The way he nodded over and over as she launched into the story of her dad even though she really had no business weighing him down with her stories. He had melted her heart when he had picked her up and rolled her around as they left the carnival, but, when she expected the hot kiss that was supposed to lead to the hot passionate sex that would be much better than the one she had watched him have with that Asian girl, he had said a courteous "goodnight" and had disappeared down the hall in the direction of his room. As she had heard his door open and close, she had been left so stranded that she wanted to burst into his room.

She still peeped at him through the hole and still watched him dress and undress. But perhaps the most exciting of all the things she watched him do was strut around his room with that long sword. She watched him cut through the air and strike different poses. The way his long legs would stretch forward and land on the floor gently like he was a chameleon one minute, and then the swift transition from being a slow walking, careful trotting chameleon to a swift fipper. Cutting through the air in ways that told her that if anyone had been within the range of that blade, they would be dead instantly. She silently watched him each time. Wondering what was it that made him so angry that he fought with himself so violently.

He was angry. She could tell that much from the way his brow knitted together anytime he was fighting in his room like that. His anger showed itself in the way his veins stood out when he held the sword. From the rippling of his biceps to the redeeming of his eyes. Even all the way through to the beads of sweat that fell from his hair to the rest of his body. Making little rivers of pain as it trailed down his body and looked around his loins.

She could see his anger in the set of his jaw and the look in his eyes. But who was he angry with?

What was the cause of this all-encompassing and all-consuming anger that he felt? Where did it come from and what could she do to ease it? Would he even let her come close enough to help? Would he even want to tell her the truth about himself?

She had gone through the past few weeks ruminating upon all these things. Wondering why he had not tried to kiss her. Was she not pretty enough? She admitted that the long jet black hair of the Asian girl was enviable.... But she also knew that she had a better face. At least she believed she did. Why did he give himself to her like that and ignored her? Why did he seem like he didn't notice how long she fumbled with her house keys? Why was he oblivious to the way she pushed her chest forward and pouted her lips while looking into his eyes?

Was he totally blind to the open invitation or had he chosen to ignore them? She was worried that perhaps he didn't even like the scent of her perfume. After all, his room had smelt of some sort of special incense when she had gone in there.

"Hm, I'll check my schedule to know if I'll be free" she had said to him. She figured that if he wanted to act like a gentleman, she had better also act like a lady. She had rushed into the room and pretended to be looking through her diary for about a minute. Then she had walked back to the door and nodded in his face.

"Yes... lunch will be good. I think I'm free tomorrow afternoon."

Now her shift was over and she could not be happier than she was at that moment. She put her cashier in order and started to get ready to leave the minute her colleague, Jon, walked into the store. She was going for a lunch date with her heartthrob.

As if on cue, Jon, her relief came into the store whistling and bidding his head around that time.

"Oh Jon, you're a darling." She exclaimed as she saw that he had come in on time. She checked herself out in the mirror and dabbled some more lipstick just so he sure that she looked perfect enough.

"You always say that Amie... You never mean it!" he called to her from the register as he looked through the sales for the day.

"I do mean it today, and just to show you how much I do, I'll bring you something tomorrow. You'll see!" he nodded unbelievingly at her and continued to do what he was doing.

When she was done checking herself out, she walked towards him and put out her hands.

"Hey... how do i look?" She asked.

"You look stunning!" Amie whirled around and her heart throb was right at the door. Watching her with admiration in his eyes.

"Oh!" she blushed all over and would have run away if she could. He walked over to her however and took her hand in his.

"Are you ready?" he asked after exchanging a polite "hello" with the surprised guy who sat behind the counter.

"Yes... yes I'm ready!" she said with the shock of his intrusion still in her face and neck.

"Alright then... let's get out of here" he said to her as he led her to the front door, while Jon watched them with a small smile of admiration on in his face.

They had barely gotten into the car before he slid in a disc to the car stereo. Next thing shc knew, Michael Jackson's Billy Jean was playing and filling up the air.

"Oh my God! You listen to Michael Jackson?" She almost yelled in delight.

"Oh yea... Jackson is a personal favourite of mine." He said as he raised his voice and started to sing along. She couldn't help but laugh.

"You have the worst singing voice ever!" she said to him and he laughed too but continued singing.

"Oh for Pete's sake stop!" she said as she covered her ears in mock horror. At this point he turned to her and said

"The only way to make me stop is to sing it better than I do"

She shook her head in disagreement.

"I don't think so. There's like a million ways I could make you stop without singing." He laughed and nodded.

"Okay... give it your best shot m'lady" she leaned closer to him, feeling particularly naughty due to

the direction their conversation had taken.
She stuck her fingers up his ribs and started to tickle. She started small and delicate and then increased it until it was nearly violent. He just continued to drive and smile.
"Hey! Do you have no sensibility at all?" she yelled at him in frustration.
"I don't know... There are other places you could touch to find out, you know" he winked at her and she blushed again. Considering how many times she had fantasized about kissing him and touching him, she felt like a complete idiot for feeling embarrassed by his statement.
He finally pulled the car to a stop outside a quiet Japanese restaurant.
"Let's go to this place. I am going to teach you how to use chopsticks!" she laughed.
"But I already know how to eat the Japanese way." He looked at her and smiled.
"So you are one of those women who think that all Asians are the same?" She frowned slightly and started to shake her head but then he cut in before

she could.

"Well... m'lady, it's my pleasure to inform you that your stereotype is wrong. Especially when it comes to body parts. Not all Asians are small in the same places." He said with a wicked grin. She almost fainted. She had never actually given it a real thought but now that she thought about it, she remembered that she had heard it said somewhere that Asian men have smaller penises. He laughed when he saw just how red she had become.

"Hey... There's no need to look like that." He said and she smiled.

"What is wrong with me?" She asked herself with a ready answer. She knew what was wrong with her and as she walked into the Chinese restaurant, she made a mental note not to let anything get to her anymore. If he wanted to be flirty, then she would be flirty too. It takes two to play that game.

He pulled her chair and she sat down. She was hardly on her seat before a handsome waiter came over to their table and took their orders.

"So tell me, what would you rather be having if not

coffee and cookies with me right now?" he asked with a mischievous smile. She shrugged and said in a light voice.

"Hotdog." his eyes widened and he couldn't hold his surprise at her obvious flirting.

"Are you for real?" He asked. She met his gaze with pouty lips and eyes blazing her desire.

"Why? You don't believe me? "

"Oh I do. I just can't believe my luck that I get to get you some hotdogs."

"Who says i'll let you get me hot dogs?" She asked with one eyebrow raised in a mocking demand.

"I don't know... I... I guess I took it for granted that you would be letting me get you the hotdogs."

She seemed to think about it for a minute and then she smiled naughtily.

"Well... I will have to check out the hot dogs anyway. Maybe if it is impressive, I'll gobble it up." his eyes widened and he tried not to choke on the coffee that he has just sipped.

"Oh my God! You're so weird!" He said as he looked away from her.

"What... I'm weird? What does that even mean?"
He shook his head and looked her in the eyes.
"I'm not sure, you just seem a little too much." he said with a wink.
"Weakling" she said under her breath and looked behind her as if something had caught her attention there.
"Excuse me? What did you say?" he asked.
"Nothing." She said with a straight face.
"Don't you dare... You said something."
"And you know this because?"
"I know because I heard you" she looked away from him a little bit.
"I said weakling!" he jerked the seat he was in backwards and stood up in a flash. He dropped some Dollar bills on the table and grabbed her by the wrist. He then half dragged her out of the place and headed for the car.
She got into the car beside him and the minute she was in, he crushed her lips with his before she could react and caught her tongue between his teeth before she could protest. He was working on her

lower lips and upper lips simultaneously, kissing and sucking with fervour. Her hand came up as if to push him away but seemed to change her mind, and the hand that had been pushing him away started to draw him to her in no time. He put in all the anger and passion that was in him, kissing her so hard that she didn't even notice his hand when it went under her dress and unclasped the bra she had on from its front hook. As if he had just changed his mind, he pulled away and started the car.

Embarrassed, she sat up and started to adjust her clothes.

"Where ... where are you going?"

"We are going home." was his brief and simple response.

She remained quiet and let him drive her home. She followed him up the stairs and as they got to her door, with her heart beating so fast, she started to try to fumble with the lock. He pulled her close and resumed the hot nerve wracking activities that they were having before he drove them home. He pulled her dress from her and his mouth found her breasts while his hands smacked her closer to him so that she could instantly feel the tumescence of him. He brought her hand to him and made her wrap her hand around it. Her touch was tentative and shy and he had to repeat the movement of clamping her hand around him to make sure that she understood that she needed to touch him as he needed to touch her. She caught on and started to rub it. She instinctively trailed her hand up and down his shaft. Making him moan gently and lift her into the air so that her legs became wrapped around his waist. Just as he started to reach for her mouth again, his phone started to ring. He hesitated and looked at her. He picked up and saw that it was a text. He put her down and opened the text. Instantly, he tensed up and looked at her.

"I'm sorry... I have to go." He said and before she could even say anything in response, he was running down the stairs. She remained there by the door, feeling like a complete idiot and wanting to cry.

Chapter 8

Amie pushed in the door and walked into the tea shop with her face averted. She was not sure why but she still felt funny about the night before. How could he abandon her like that? What was it that was so important that he had to leave her in the bed and disappear into the night? Where did he go? What did he do? Was the call from that other woman? Did he really prefer her to him?

A part of her was angry. And another part of her was just sad. All of her life, she had been used to men trying to take advantage of her. Men trying to use her for their own pleasure. Men who looked at her and only saw something to conquer, something to subdue. Perhaps the fact that she remained a virgin had something to do with the fact that she was often irritated by them. Their manners, their attitudes, everything about them generally anyway. She had made it a point to avoid such men and to only go out with people that she perceived as decent. Now for the first time in her life, her urge to make love and feel the touch of a man was looming greater than her irritation for self-indulgent takers. And for the first time in her life, she was being incessantly turned down. Somewhere inside her, she felt sad that it would be this sort of time of all times that she would experience this sort of thing.

Presently, she sat down at a corner, and when Amanda approached her table with a smile, thinking that it was one of her other customers, she fought hard to return the smile.

"Girl... what will you have?" Amanda asked with an attitude. Amie frowned and nodded at the menu. As Amanda walked away, Amie noticed three men walking into the place. They didn't seem to be together but somehow, she had a feeling that they were together and she grew highly suspicious of them.

There was something going on in the news. One of the old men who had been there that first day when Amie walked into the place was there, staring at it and mumbling to himself.

"Say Amanda could you give this thing some

volume?"

"Go get your own damn T.V Joe and don't bother me!" she yelled at him but one of the three scary looking men turned to her and nodded at the T.V. "increase the damn volume!" he said with an accent thick that one could cut through it with a knife. She obviously didn't like people coming into her shop and telling her what to do but then she had also noticed how dangerous he looked. She increased the TV volume and Amie's attention was drawn to the news. Three faces were shown in relation to a murder that occurred the night before and her eyes nearly popped out of its socket as she recognized the lady who had been in Shin's room the other time. The lady with the long hair and slim body. She was one of the dead people alongside two other men. Amie nearly jumped out of her chair as she realized that the time frame of the murders was in line with the time he left her and the time she later heard his door open and closed.

"Did Shin kill these people? Did he leave her in bed to go on a killing spree? Did he abandon her in that bed because he wanted to kill the woman he had been in bed with only recently? What was all this all about?" Her heart raced as she wondered if she was fraternising with a murderer. She wondered if she had been spot on when she had been afraid of him when he had talked about poisons. Was it just her imaginations or was it starting to look like the man who lived next door to her was a cold blooded killer? Her phone pinged and she reluctantly checked it. It was Shin. She looked at the phone for a minute, trying to decide if she should reply him or not.

"Well... he hasn't done anything to me to make me ignore him. Besides... if he wanted me dead, I most likely would be dead anyway." She thought to herself as she picked up her phone and responded to him.

"Hi..." she answered.

"Hey sorry about last night. I had some really urgent business to attend to." He said.

"Oh yea?" she said inside her before typing "It's okay."

"Well... I was wondering if you wouldn't mind me

making it up to you. Let's have a cup of coffee together." She thought about it for a minute and decided that there was no harm in it. After all, if this was about intimidating her or scaring her, there were like a hundred ways he could have done that without needing to invite her to coffee first.

"Sure... I'm at Amanda's. Can you come over there?" he wasn't responding anymore. Now what was his problem this time? Was he coming or going or was he just going to have her sit there and wait for him without showing up?

"You know what... I'll give him ten minutes. If he is not here in ten, I'm out of here!" she said to herself as she sat back and started to mentally count the minutes until he would show up.

"I'm taking a big risk here. What if this guy is just a serial killer? What am I going to do if he attacks me?" It was a question that had kept on roaming around her mind since she had heard him talk about trust and poisons like that. Now it was starting to look to her like she needed to make up her mind and make it up fast. If he really was killer, one of the last things she wanted to do was let him know that she knew about him. But how was she to remain normal if she knew that the man seated across from her was a killer?

His words from the other night came back to her. When he said he wasn't a saint, did he really mean to tell her that he was a demon and that she should be wary of him? When he told her that he had done some bad things in his own time, did he really mean that he had killed more people than he could count? She dropped her head in her palms and closed her eyes, a part of her wanted to believe that Shin was a gentle man. That he was a good guy and would never attack anyone unless first attacked. But then the other part of her, the part that was logical enough to know that the death of the woman who had been in his bed with two other Asian looking men from a katana was not going to be a coincidence to the fact that he just happened to own a katana and practiced with it so often. There really could only be so many coincidences. She silently started to feel like calling her mom. Just in case this man decided that he wanted her dead, she needed to talk to her mom one last time at least. She was still pondering on whether she should step out for a moment and call her mother or just wait for Shin to arrive, talk to him and then call her mother later. Before she could make up her mind, he walked into the room, looking like he was ready to take on the whole world or something.

"Hi..." he said with a small smile."

"Hi" she answered back in the same manner.

"I'm sorry about last night..." he said again and she nodded. Now that she looked at him, she could see that he wasn't the sort that she had feared that he was. His eyes were soft and his lips looked ready to be kissed. For a moment, all she wanted to do was drag him back home and make him finish what they had started the night before.

"Well, how was your day been?" he asked her. She frowned and nodded slightly.

"It has been fine but for the news of three people murdered in the streets last night." she said while looking into his eyes fixedly.

"Oh... that's too bad. It is becoming more dangerous out there every day." She was staring into his eyes, hoping that somehow he would see that she suspected him of the murders. He however didn't seem to notice and he beckoned to Amanda instead and ordered his own cup of coffee. Amanda seemed really happy to serve him and she was back with his coffee in moment. As he picked up the coffee mug that had been placed in front of him, he exposed his wrist and Amie's eyes caught a rather deep wound that looked fresh on the inner side of his wrist. Her eyes widened. Before that moment, all she had was speculations, but now, at that moment, she was looking at proof that he had been in a violent tussle recently. If one added the fact that three people who she thought he knew were dead, what she really had was a gruesome picture. She was sitting across from a murderer. A man who had taken other human's lives! Her confusion and fear travelled from her mind to her hands and her hands reacted to that by shaking violently. Suddenly, she spilled the coffee she was trying to bring to her lips.

"Are you okay?" he asked as he started to help her dry off with paper towels. She shook her head and looked into his eyes.

"Yea... I guess..." and then before she could get the chance to think about it,

"What happened to your wrist?" she asked as she nodded at the bruised wrist. He looked at it and then at her. Then he smiled.

"Last night.... I was visiting some friends and this happened. It happens a lot." He said with a smile. He even threw in a bout of nervous laughter for good measure. She continued to stare at him. Obviously, she did not believe him one bit.

"Common... it is funny... what's up with you today?" he asked with a slight frown. She looked at him in that moment and decided that if she must die, she would die just once. She decided to confront him with the question directly

"Shin... did you kill those people?"

He didn't look shocked by her question. Rather, he looked like he had been expecting it. He looked into her eyes and stared at her as if he was contemplating what to tell her and how it would be best to tell it to her. Before he could make up his mind, she added.

“Think about the response very well Shin... I am no police officer or private investigator but I can put two and two together. You left me abruptly last night and returned about three hours later, I don’t believe it’s a coincidence people died within that time frame too and you show up with a cut this morning. But please, tell me I'm wrong. Tell me this was just a mix up and you did not actually kill those people!” the panic in her voice was palpable and she was starting to shake. Her eyes were red and she looked like she would bring the whole building down with a really loud scream.

"Amie... calm yourself. There is an explanation for everything.” She shook her head and started to push her chair away from him.

“That woman was with you and I saw her that night. I saw the two of you together and now she is dead. Is that what is going to happen to me too? Am I going to just wind up dead? It does seem like people around you seem to get into trouble doesn't it?" she was shouting now and the people in the shop were watching her. They were watching them. He remained in his seat, looking like he was going to pounce on her and stuff things in her mouth to keep her quiet.

She continued to talk in fast tones. Not seeming to notice that his eyes were roving around the room and seeming to notice things around her. He closed his eyes for a minute as if willing himself to be calm. But her voice continued to float to him, her complaints and her fear. Eventually, he looked up into her eyes and said to her in his harshest voice yet.

"Goddamn it Amie, shut up!" she was stunned by the way he yelled at her. For a few seconds, she was quiet. Then she opened her mouth to say something but instead her mouth hung open.

"There is no point in screaming that loud my friend!" Amie and Shin whirled around and looked in the direction of the voice.

"Long time no see my dear friend." The man said.

Most of his face was shrouded by a face cap but from Shin's reaction, it was obvious that he knew who it was. They were both silent, looking at each other as if they were in some sort of a stare down with the difference being that the other man was not really looking because the face cap covered his face. Amie cleared her throat in hopes that it would bring them both to their senses as she could already feel the tension of a bull about to charge.

For the first time she was noticing the men who had joined them in the coffee shop while she was carried away with worrying about the dead people. She frowned at first, and was about to tell the intruding man that this was none of his business when Shin pushed her to the floor with a loud

"Get down Amie!" she hit the ground with a thud just as the first sound of gunshots rung in the air. It was sudden and it was unexpected and unanticipated. The bullets started to fly and all of a sudden, she saw Shin bring out two guns from his pockets and start to shoot at their attackers. There were six men in all and they covered each other such that he could not turn away from any of them even for a minute without getting hit.

Crouched beneath the tables, Amie was shaking like a tree in a storm as she watched shell casings and bullets clatter to the floor like rain drops. The iron table that they had been at shielded them from the bullets for the moment but the rain of pullets on it was starting to dent it and she was starting to wonder how long it would hold against these men who were determined to kill them.

“Oh my God! Oh my God!” she was screaming under the table where she was plastered to the floor. Away from the view of the men who had invaded Amanda's shop and were now shooting the place up.

“I knew I would get in trouble with this guy! I just didn’t know it would be this sort of trouble!” she exclaimed to herself quietly. “What am I ever going to do now?” she looked around the room for some sort of escape route but noticed that all exits were blocked by armed men.

Seeing that there was no way out of the place, she

lay down and stayed the way Shin had pushed her. Shin didn't seem to be seeing her at that moment as he was too engrossed in a gun battle with the men. The sound of bullets hitting different things all around her was scary. She waited mentally for one of them to hit him but minute after minute; she found that the fight was not going to end so fast.

Finally, she heard the clicking of empty guns. They were out of bullets. To some extent, this was a good thing for her, but then in other aspects and dimensions, it was not so much of a good news. The fact that there were no more bullets meant that they were going to have to fight within close range. She peeped around the table to see that two men out of the six men that had been in the room were down. One of them had been shot in the head and his eyes were open as he stared blankly into space. The other man was face down and she couldn't really tell from where she was if he was dead or alive. She also couldn't tell what part of his body had been shot.

Shin slid cautiously out from behind his table refuge. He approached the men with some caution just before he got to them. He slid a dagger out of his pocket before they could see it and the man that had been rushing at him was stabbed in the neck. He must have hit the carotid artery because blood started to splatter all over the room. The blood was shooting into the air and landing in whatever direction the bleeding man turned that side of his neck. From Amie's angle, she was already soaked with the dying man's blood, and when he fell down about two minutes after he started to run around the room confused and scared of what was happening to him, she started to vomit all over him even as he shook in the last vibrations before he would be dead. She could not help it. A mixture of coffee and pasta that she had had for breakfast kept spurting out of her mouth and all over the place. In horror of what she was doing, she fell back away from him. The katana sword that the man was holding fell from his hand and Shin had grabbed it mid air. Her fear was palpable and she was whimpering but Shin almost couldn't hear her. He seemed to have been transported to another part of the world, another pan of existence at that point. Using one of the still standing tables as a propeller, Shin jumped through the air and landed right in the middle of two out of the remaining three men. He hit the first man with the butt of the katana he was holding. The man fell back a little, stunned and confused from the force of the katana. Then Shin turned his back on him and turning in a 180 degree turn, he faced the other man while instantly stooping to avoid the dagger that had been thrown at him by the man who was standing a little way away from him. The katana slashed through the nearby man's legs and with an almost inhuman cry of pain, he fell to the ground as his legs had been cut off from under him neat. Shin abandoned him for the minute and turned to the man who had thrown the dagger, and was now running towards him with his own sword drawn and ready to run through Shin. From where Amie now stood watching the events, she screamed.

"Shin!" he turned and leaned out of the way such that the other man's katana sword ran through the air and buried itself in the chair behind him instead. Shin brought his sword up into the air and with what seemed to be a war cry, he brought it down on the man just right between his neck and shoulder blade. The man was instantly on the ground, shaking in the last throes of death. Shin screamed "Arrrgah" and turned on the man whose legs he had chopped off. The man, seeing that Shin was approaching to finish him off, started to laugh. He was giggling through the enormous pain that he was going through at that moment.

"You are still Viper; you will always be Viper!" the man was saying through his giggles. Shin looked at him, as he came close to him to finish him off, the giggling man smiled with blood spattered all over his face.

"I am what I am..." Shin said with a blank face.

"They will find you... "Shin moved closer to the man and looked into his eyes.

"Maybe they will. But it won't be a dog like you that will kill me." With this, Shin put the sword through the man's chest and must have pierced through the heart because the man then fell backwards in a matter of seconds. Shin then walked over to where Amie was seated in a pool of her own vomit.

"We need to get out of here!" he said and for the first time, she noticed the sound of the sirens that cut through the silence. The police were near. Shin led her through a back door that led through the kitchen. On the way out of the place, they found Amanda on the floor, passed out and fainted on the floor. Sadie wondered at what point she had fainted. At the level of the gunshots or after they had started the dagger and Katana fight.

He took her through some dark alleys as they were both soaked with blood and would have been easily detected if they walked through the streets. For the first time she had moved into her apartment building, she walked through the backdoor into the house. He took her up the stairs and walked her to her door. All through the walk, he had been quiet and almost cold. He had held her hand loosely without any emotion. She had stolen glances at him from time to time but she could not see anything in his eyes. Just a cold blankness like the one that one would find if they looked down at a dry well in winter. Her lips trembled from the impact of the experience she had just had and her blood pressure must have risen because she was suddenly having this splitting headache.

“What now?” she asked herself more than once as they walked to the house and she had been unable to answer it. She knew that he definitely would not be staying nearby. He would need to get as far away from the place as he could. If the police arrested him, she would be sad. But she couldn’t even tell at that point which would be worse, having the police arrest him, or having those men get their hands on him. What was she to do now? How was she to hide him? And how was she to be safe anyway?

“Here... go in your house and lock the door. Clean up and stay out of sight for as long as you can...” he paused for a minute and looked at her coldly.

“You were right. If a woman stays with me, she might be in danger. I don’t want you to be in any more danger than what you have already experienced." She started to shake her head. She wanted to tell him to take her with him but she didn't want to sound clingy. This was not about being clingy, she was afraid that they might come back for her and then she might not have him to defend her. She was afraid that now that they knew the place she stayed, they might come back and kill her or torment her. She wanted to leave too but how far could she go really?

"Shin..." she started to say something. She wanted to tell him that she didn't feel safe without him in that house. She wanted to tell him that she was sorry for talking to him so harshly. She wanted to tell him to take her with him, but she cut her short.

"Good bye Amie. You will not be seeing me again."

And he was gone. She stood at the door for what seemed like ten years but was really ten minutes, and when she finally closed the door behind her, she fell to the floor of her room and burst into tears.

Chapter 9

The days after Shins disappearance saw her

cowering in her room and refusing to get out. On one hand, she was afraid that if she stepped out, she might be recognised by someone who had seen what happened and reported to the police, while on the other hand, she was afraid that the men who were hunting Shin had not really left town totally and that she would be at their mercy if they caught her and recognised her. She wanted to stay on a low key for as long as possible as Shin had instructed, and she even wondered how Amanda had not talked to the police yet. She figured that if Amanda talked to the police, she would be arrested and charged with conspiracy or any such thing that fit their description of what she had done. She had seen a whole lot of movies where the police had the situation all wrong and arrested the wrong people just because they had wrong information or they had been influenced by the people who were hunting the characters. One night, she had thought that she heard something downstairs and had been frozen in a corner of her room for as long as she thought whatever it was still there.

She would look in the peep hole over and over again, hoping to catch a glimpse of the man. She willed all her experiences of the last few days to be just some bad dream. She willed it to be some sort of hanky-panky on the part of her mind. Some sort of hallucination that would soon wear off. But the more she peeped into the hole every day, she discovered that she was not hallucinating at all, and that Shin and his godlike body and spirit like moves were gone for good. Her heart sank every morning when she thought about the things that she had lost. That feeling of loss was back again.

The feeling she had finally gotten as she watched her father's body being lowered into the floor. The feeling she had seen in her mother's eyes. That feeling of loneliness and emptiness. She could feel it now even worse than ever. When she had buried her father, she had thought that somehow it was some sort of relief. Especially since she would not see him suffer so much anymore. He would not come home with bleeding wounds and broken bones anymore. Neither would he be coming home with injured organs and ruptured spleen. It seemed to her that death was the ultimate rest and after a while, she had stopped feeling abandoned and left alone. She had started to feel like now he would be okay forever.

With Shin, it was different.

She could not stop grieving. She could not tell if he was dead or not. She could not tell if he was safe or was being tortured by someone. She felt like he had abandoned her, like he had left her to the mercies of whatever would come for her. Suddenly, the building seemed to have become menacing and dangerous without him in it. She constantly wondered if she would fall off the stairs or if she would be attacked by some wild animal that had been lurking in the walls all the while. Waiting to get their slimy grimy hands on her. She walked with caution and made sure she didn't make any noise, she now used the backdoor downstairs more often. The last thing she wanted was to be snatched by people who would kill her like she saw all those other men die.

"Oh common... be serious. You are not their target. Shin is." She would say to herself sometimes because she wanted to be less afraid but somehow, she knew that if they had been able to kill Shin that day, she wouldn't have been spared. She would have died alongside him. She knew that even if they knew that they were just neighbours who happened to be friendly, they might have killed her just to spite him. Now, as she moved through the motions of her life, reading the news and seeing the headlines declaring that the police had come to a dead end on the Asian men's case, she knew that she would do well to get out of the town as soon as she finished her course.

Three weeks have passed since then. She received a text message. She looked at her phone screen and frowned. It had been a while since she received a text on her phone. When she opened it, it was Shin.

"Amie... lets meet. It's urgent. Coffee shop!"

The text read. She couldn't believe her eyes. Shin was alive! And he wasn't just alive, he was in town. She had thought that he would be half way across the world by that time. She had thought that he would have forgotten about her and probably moved on and starting a new life with some other girl now. She had thought it was time for her to move on too and try to build a life without Shin.

"Oh my god!" she exclaimed. A wave of feelings washed over her as she thought about what he must have gone through in the last three weeks. Was he in town for good? Had he come to take her with him? Did he just need help with something? Her heart raced as she hurriedly pulled on her jacket and picked up her phone and purse.

"He abandoned you... should you be rushing out to see him so fast? Shouldn't you give him some attitude at least?" a part of her asked.

"He didn't abandon me. He had to go. He didn't have a choice. Besides... I was safer here than if I was with him." she was making excuses for him and she knew it but she couldn't help it. Now that he was around and needed her, she was not about to deny him whatever he needed.

"You're just lying!" she said to herself but she was

not listening anymore. She stepped into the street and half ran and half walked to the coffee shop.

She pushed the door open and walked in and noticed instantly that the room had not been used in a while. The blood had been cleaned but she could still see the faces of all of the men who had died there in her head. There were still the pools of blood and holes in the walls in her mind and she suddenly felt a wave of nausea. She walked into the kitchen area and remembered how she had seen Amanda on the floor passed out. She felt sorry for Amanda. She could only imagine how she must be feeling, especially with her shop shot up and the people killed in it. It was obvious to her the shop would not be coming back into business anytime soon.

The woman had seemed like a pretty nice person. She did not deserve to have her shop ruined like that. Amie made a mental note to volunteer if she ever opened the coffee shop again. She would work for free just to show the woman that she was sorry and help her get back on feet. She looked around at the damages and came face to face with a rather huge spider web. In the three weeks since the place had been empty of humans, the place was fast gaining new occupants. She brushed the webs off her face angrily and looked around again. This time, she was looking for Shin. He ought to be here by now? What did he think he was? Abandoning her only to show up three weeks later and request to meet and then come late to the meeting point?

"Where is this Shin?" she said aloud after she had walked through the place looking for him but seeing that he was not anywhere in sight.

"Right here baby!" she turned around fast and saw instantly that she had been deceived. It was not Shin who stood there but another Asian looking man. She turned and started to run towards the exit but she slammed into two other men who stood in her way.

"Well... isn't she pretty!" one man said as she saw them closing in on her.

"Uuuggghhh! Not even one bit. She is ugly as fuck" the other man said as the all closed in on her. There seemed to be about ten of them.

“Yes... she is very ugly.” Another said.

“Oh common guys... You have to admit that Shin has good tastes. This one doesn’t look so bad” another chipped in.

“Excuse me? Can you see her nose? She looks like a tortoise!” one man exclaimed. Tired and angry with his colleagues for the way they were starting to debate about the girl, the man who had spoken first said with anger in his voice.

“Well... who cares? She will be very dead by the time we are done with her.”

The men burst into laughter and it was all she could do to not burst into tears. She suddenly realized that she should have known better. If he had really wanted to see her, Shin would have known how to find her and not have to resort to an anonymous text.

“Oh God! I'm so screwed” She said to herself as the men drew closer. She was looking around. Realizing that her only escape would be to call the attention of passersby, she raised her voice and screamed as loud as she could. The scream was barely out of her mouth when a hand covered her mouth and a handkerchief was held over mouth and nose. By the third gulp for air, she knew that she was not going to be escaping this. The blackness of unconsciousness beckoned towards her and she did not have the strength to fight it. Before the fight had even started, she surrendered to the effects of whatever it is that the cloth had been soaked in.

The room was dark and hazy. Or was it just her mind playing tricks on her? She stirred, or tried to stir but discovered that she was bound hands and feet. She had been coming out of the sleep gently before but now she woke up with a start.

In a flash, the events that led to her capture replayed themselves through her mind and she was brought up to speed in a jiffy. She looked around the room, wide eyes and half surprised that she had not been killed. What did these men want? Why did they take her? What did they hope to get from taking her? She swallowed hard and discovered that her throat was parched. She needed water. How long had she been in that room exactly? She looked around again

"Hello!" She tried to scream but only a hoarse sound came out of her. She cleared her throat and screamed again and this time, she was able to make a good sound.

"Hello!" She was hoping that someone would hear her and come and give her some water at least. A door opened in the far end of the room she looked in the direction and saw a man walking in. He was one of the men that had taken her from the coffee shop.

"Hey... sleeping beauty... actually, sleeping ugly!" the man said as he came close to her and lifted her chin with his fingers.

"Please... I need water. I am thirsty!" she said with appeal in her eyes. He looked like he was about to burst into laughter for a moment but then he calmed down and looked at her.

"What makes you think I care if you are thirsty?" he asked. She swallowed hard again and her throat hurt badly.

"Well... I guess I would be dead if you wanted me dead" she said. He nodded quietly and looked at her.

"The ugly girl is kinda smart!" he said with an evil smile.

"Please... just give me some water." She said again. Hoping that she would be able to appeal to his good side before the rest came in and collectively decided her fate. He shook his head and gave her a very evil grin.

"Naaa... not wanting you dead yet does not mean that we want to pamper you. You deserve all the torture you can get." She almost burst into tears because just then, before she could even try to persuade him anymore, the rest came in one after the other.

"But what did he ever do to you? What is Shin's offence to make me deserve all this? What did he ever do wrong?" the men in the room looked at her with surprise on her face.

"So he never even told you anything about himself?"

one of them asked her with mockery in his voice.

"We are not that close." She answered with a shrug.

"But he likes you. We can see it. We know he will come here to try to rescue you and that is when we will make him pay for all he has done to the family."

"Family? What Family? Are you all his siblings? What did he do to his family?" she was starting to get agitated. Perhaps it had something to do with the fact that she was dehydrated.

"Calm down girl. We are not biological siblings, but we all belong to a single clan called "the blood dragons." We are one of the biggest business organizations in Japan and we control the politics, the streets, the drugs, the prostitutes, the money basically. We used to also do some dry cleaning jobs once in a while." She looked at him with wide eyes.

"Dry cleaning?" She asked with surprise written all over her voice. What did dry cleaning have to do with the obvious organized crime gang that they were running? The men saw her confusion and laughed loudly.

"Well... we clean out people who stand in our way

or in the way of people who are ready to pay us to do it." One of the men said with a smile. He then ran a hand over her chest tentatively.

"People like you..." another man said.

"Shin was known as the Viper. He was the deadliest of us all and was so good at making deaths look like accidents. But he was best known for his temper. It was so bad that if anyone made him angry, he would strike them down hard and fast like a Viper. That was how he got the name Viper" she was looking at them with open mouthed awe now.

"But it wasn't his abilities alone that endeared him to the master..." one man said.

"No... it was also his dogged loyalty. Shin was so loyal that when the master placed the katana in his hands and asked him to cut his best friend, he did it without hesitation. He would still be in the graces of the master if not for the war with 'cobra 69' ... I know it for sure."

Now her head was reeling. What the hell was a cobra 69? She looked up at the man who had first come into the room.

"What is cobra 69?" she asked with a puzzled expression.
"It is another clan, more like another organization. We had a row out with them and master sent Shin to deal with their leader. He was supposed to infiltrate them and kill their leader..."
"Then he met that girl..." at the mention of the word 'girl', her ears perked up like a dogs and she looked up at them.
"Girl?" she asked. More like exclaimed.
"Ohhhhhhhh" the men chorused.
"You like him too! Perfect!"
"What girl?" she repeated. But one of the men slapped her hard across the face, her cheeks became pink and he pulled at her shirt. The buttons of the shirt were sent flying in different directions in the room. She looked up.
"What ... what are you doing?" she screamed but the men only laughed and touched her all over. One of the men continued the story.
"He met the master of the cobra 69's daughter and fell in love with her. They could not hold back. He

could not carry out his master's order anymore. So the master ordered the clan to kill both of them. We raped her and took her head right there in front of him. It was a successful mission and we left after driving the katana through him. We thought he was dead but obviously, he wasn't. Two months later, he came back and killed master and over sixty members of the blood dragons..."

"Then he burnt our temples to the ground and left a message telling us that we would meet god too if we searched for him. This was like a dare. We had to take it. And so here we are"

Suddenly the single bulb that served as light in the room went out and a couple of 'oh's and 'ah's from frustrated men who really wanted to defile her and it over with.

"Go check on the light, black scorpion." One man said amongst them. The man who had been referred to as black scorpion grumbled and started to move in the direction of the light switch. As he walked away from the point where they were trying totals Amie, a swoosh was heard and then the man screamed in agony and the next thing they Knew, he was on the floor in front of them. His throat had been slit from ear to ear and he was doing the final dance of death. Jerking in a horizontal manner that put fear in the heart of everyone present. They all stood up and scrambled for their swords but even as they rushed around, two more men dropped dead and the remaining four ran into a corner hoping for cover.

From above the ceiling, Amie watched a rope like object descend towards them and then swung straight at them in that corner. It had moved so fast that none of them had seen what it was until it was buried in the heart of one of them. Even Amie started to shake in fear especially since she did not know who it was that was attacking them. She did not know if it was Shin who had come to rescue her or some other person who just wanted to kill everyone. She didn't know if she was going to be one of the dead people by the time the person was done or if she would be spared and allowed to go back home in peace. Even if she wanted to run, she couldn't because both her hands and legs were bound and she was unable to move around. She kept her eyes closed as she didn't want to see any more people die right in front of her eyes. For alloy the ills that they had done to her, she hated to see them all die so gruesomely. Besides, who was to tell her that she was going to survive it all either?

“Shin... I know you are there... Show yourself and stop being cowardly!” One of them, the one who appeared to be the leader said with a loud voice. The room was deathly quiet and she could suddenly hear the birds outside chirping. She was sure that if a pin was dropped in that moment, she would have heard it clatter to the ground. The three men huddled together, looking scared but holding onto their swords firmly. She could not see their faces, but at that moment, she felt like a bloodhound, perceiving their fear and their sweat mixed with the blood of their comrades all over the place. She could tell that the men believed that the person they were up against was Shin. She still couldn't be sure. She didn't want to raise her hopes just in case it turned

out that they were wrong. She didn't want to rely on what those men thought that was happening.
The silence of the room suddenly became shattered as one of the men screamed out loud again. Amie couldn't see what had happened to him.
Again, Amie could not really see him. She really couldn't tell how the mystery killer achieved this feat but the man that was dangling from the roof was evidence that it could be done.
Finally, there was only the leader standing, the one whom she had begged for water. The light suddenly came back on and she was treated to the gory sight of the men who were littered all over the floor and the ceiling. Her hands, though tied started to shake at the violence that stood before her. Suddenly, one of the asbestos ceilings in the room caved open and Shin jumped down. He was dressed in all black and looked like he had lost a whole lot of weight. She watched him warily and semi angrily. She was mostly naked and her hair was basically the only thing covering her up. A rage of different emotions washed through her as she wondered if she should

just scream at him and attack him with her nails once he freed her or to just pick up the shreds of her clothing and dignity and leave the town forever. But there was still business to be settled. He walked over to where the leader stood and looked into his face.

"I heard that you are the new master's errand boy..." He said to the man who now stood with his katana drawn and his face expressionless.

"Don't worry... It is a good job if you are working for a good master. But the Blood dragon..." He shook his head gently.

"I don't think that is a good place to be a servant."

The man looked at him with contempt in his eyes and shook his head.

"I am not a servant. I am a brother..." Shin laughed at this. He seemed genuinely amused

"I thought the same. But as I came to find out, it wasn't so. Not in the least."

"Let's get this over with. It will be an honour to me to be the one to take your head to the master. I will particularly love it." Again, Shin laughed at the

man.
"Of course it will be. But have you ever stopped to wonder if it happens the other way around? What if I kill you? Will all this have been worth it? Is one man's greed enough motivation and justification for your death?" Shin was trying to convince the man not to fight. This bit was obvious but the man did not seem to be getting the point as he took a step towards Shin in warning.
"Stop preaching to me. If you are afraid of me, then say so. I promise I will give you a quick death. And her too... Though I cannot promise you that she will not get a full dose of me before I take her head." it was all the motivation that Shin needed to fight. Shin drew his Katana and stood at ease. The other man rushed at him with sword stretched out. Shin raised his own sword in defence but it was a little too late and he lost his balance. He landed on the floor with a thud. The other man saw his chance and pounced on Shin.
"You are getting weak Shin... Western girls aren't doing you a whole lot of good, is it?" Shin pushed

him off him and the man rushed back at him, hoping for a repeat of what had just happened but Shin was ready this time and he met the assault with his own. The two of them were soon embattled in a hot swords fight. They pranced around the floors of the room, meeting aggression with aggression, and offence with offence and over the next twenty minutes, they battled. Amie could see that Shin was not quite in the condition to be fighting. He still hadn't healed completely from the wounds that she had helped him tend. She could see that he was slowly tiring and what the other man lacked in skill, he had in a lot of stamina. She started to struggle to free herself from the ropes that had been used to tie her. Slowly but surely, she twisted her hands around and soon one was free. Then the other, the second her other hand was free, she set to freeing her legs. She did it within minutes also and rushed across the room to get a Katana that had been dropped by one of the dead men. She picked it up and almost dropped it as she realized just how heavy it was. She realized that it would take iron of this weight too cut through flesh and bone so cleanly as Shin did at the coffee shop. The weapon was too heavy, it was not something that she could wield and she had to drop it and go for a dagger instead.

“Hey you!” She called out to the two men fighting. Shin had already seen her and her efforts to get free of her bondage. He had seen it all and had known the minute she had been free. He had seen her when she tried to wield the Katana and would have laughed if not for the fact that he was in the middle of a fight. The other man however looked in her direction when she called out and that was Shins opportunity to do him in., Shin raised the sword into the air and brought it down on the man's neck with all the strength left in him. The head rolled out onto the floor and Amie watched it with wide eyes for a moment. Then Shin put his hand in her shoulder and said to her.

“Come... Let's get the hell out of here.” He removed his shirt and wrapped it around her. Then he bent low and lifted her to his shoulder. He left the room without looking back.

Chapter 10

She was conscious. But she wished she wasn't. The thoughts of the things that had happened to her in the last ten hours made her wonder if she would ever be able to see life like a normal human anymore. The deaths, those who wanted to rape her. There was no question about it; she knew that she would not be normal for a very long time.

He was silent throughout the walk that took them to the place where an old SUV was waiting for them. What was he thinking? Did he blame her for bringing him back? Had he ever actually left the town at all? How did he even know where to come? If he knew nowhere to come, why did he take so long and practically waited till she was about to be defiled before he jumped in and started acting like a hero? She had been unconscious for a long time. She knew this because her body felt so dry. She was ravenous and shaking from the impact of the hunger in her. In spite of the fact that she was being carried, she felt like she was so tired. Too tired to be carried and too tired to be moved. She let her hands hang freely over his shoulders and watched them as they dangled from side to side. Sometimes, she would close her eyes but her eyelids also felt too heavy to be closed and then when she opened them, she would feel like her eyes would pop out of the sockets if she kept the open like that. From the way he carried her and the way he walked with her on his shoulder, it was obvious to her that he was also tired. Perhaps not quite as tired as she was, but he was definitely fatigued. Thus when he got to the car and dropped her in it, nave was glad that they had all survived the part severe he had to put her on his shoulder and walk for minutes unending. She couldn't see the environment but she could see that the area was a little wooded and that the house from which they had emerged had been isolated. When wanted to ask him

"Where are we?" But she refrained from talking. Partly because she was too tired to start a

conversation but also because she didn't think he would want to answer questions at that moment.
He dropped her; more like dumped her in the backseat and went to the driver's seat to do the driving. When he started the car, she thought she heard a screech but couldn't be sure because she was so tired and sleepy. The car surged forward and she smuggled into the back seat. Folding herself like a baby still in the uterus. From time to time, he looked back at her and tried to check on her, but he knew it was more important for him to get her to a safe place and nurse her.
What was he thinking when he left her? He asked himself as he sped through the gathering night. She had been so nice to him and he had known that the gang members had seen them together. What was he thinking? She had been alone in the house and he had thought he could watch her and make sure she was safe through the cameras that he installed in the hallway. He had thought that she was not really connected to him and that she would be relatively safe out if he left the environment but it

had turned out that he was deceiving himself. They had come back for her and knowing that he would have rigged the house against them, they had blurred her out of the building instead.

What if she had died?

She would have been the third woman who would have died because they were associated with her. He was still yet to forgive himself for letting the first two die and now they were going to add one more to the pile?

"Hell no" he muttered under his breath in Japanese and turned into a lone stretch of road. It was done. He was not going to let anyone mess his life upon anymore. He was going to defend the people he cared for. He had failed once, he was not about to let it happen again.

As he drove, he let his mind roam to the beautiful face of the woman he had loved. She had risked everything to be with him. He could remember that night, in the bed. He had wanted to tell her the truth. But how was he supposed to tell her that he really belonged to the blood dragons and that he had been sent in specifically to kill her parents and her? How was he to explain to her that he had come into her father's compound and made her love him just because he wanted to be close enough for the family to have their guard down around him so that he could kill them in cold blood? His master had taught him how to fight to kill, his master had taught him how to kill like a lion and strike like a viper. But he had taught himself how to get close to his enemies first and gain their trust before slaughtering them without remorse or mercy. He had taught himself how to make himself important to his prey such that no matter what angle his prey ran to, it would have to come back to him.

"Then I met her!" It was not a sentence of praise and neither was it derogatory. It was a sentence of surrender. He had lost himself and fallen in love. And much worse, she had loved him back. He had looked into her eyes and seen in them his future and the future of his entire lineage. He had not been worried when he took her in his arms and gently planted his seed within her.

That day, he had decided that he would tell her the truth.

As he held her close and stroked her hair, he had contemplated how to start the conversation when he felt the first sting of the needle. He didn't need to look at it to know what it was. It was either laced with poison or something else to incapacitate him. He had sprung out of bed, hoping to put up some fight before he finally died or became paralyzed but the drug was too fast. It could have brought down an elephant. He fell back into the bed and the blood dragons came in. His eyes remained open as part of the paralysis. He was not even able to move his eyelid to a shut position as they took turns on her. He watched it all.

For some reason, he knew that he wouldn't have closed his meters even if he could have. He knew that he needed to see it all so that he could avenge her properly if he ever survived the experience.

By the time the seventh man was standing from her, she looked pretty dead anyway. She was not moving, not screaming and not thrashing around anymore. Her eyes too remained open even though she had not been paralyzed. With emptiness, her beautiful hazel eyes stared into the depth of his own.

Those eyes

He still had nightmares about them.

Now he knew that he might have to start the fight all over again. His anger had been aroused again and he was going to vent. He didn't care what happened afterwards, all he knew was that people had to die. It had been over three years and he was still raw and wounded. He was still sore all over and he was still looking into those eyes in every minute of his sleep. When they had driven the Katana through him, he had thought that he was done. That he would die now and would never get a chance at his revenge.

But then he had woken up in that silent room. The katana was gone and his wounds were bandaged. He had looked around and wondered who had helped him out.

She had nursed him back to health and had helped

him get money to get out of Japan.

"Go... Go far away Viper.., don't come back. Don't look back. Save yourself." He had nodded like he was going to obey her. She had watched him get on the train but before she got back to the clan home, over sixty clan members were dead, and their master with them.

Then, and only then had he left Japan.

Now she was dead too. Her only offence was in helping him out.

He parked the car and rushed to the passenger seat. He picked her up out of the place and raced towards a fountain that sat at the centre of a beautiful garden. He placed her into it and let the water wash all over her body. He didn't bother to take the clothes off her, he just held her there till she started to stir. One eye fluttered open and the other followed suit. He sighed in relief. Two days without food and water had to be a lot of stress. He brought her out of the water when he was sure that she was adequately rejuvenated and sitting by the fountain,

he placed her on his lap and held her there.
Slowly, she started to feel better and even looked around her for the first time. It was a garden. Or at least it looked like a garden. The trees stood tall and even in the dark; they cast shadows over the whole environment. She noticed the numerous flowers that adorned the whole place in rows and roads of beautifully colourful petals. The light of the moon, though bright was shielded by the numerous tall trees that seemed to be backing like protective big brothers to the smaller plants and protecting them from the jealous stare of the moon. In a place not too far away from where she was seated in his lap, she could hear the sound of turkeys or ducks or some other similar birds crooning.
"What is this place?" She asked. Voicing the thoughts that had started to chase themselves around her mind immediately she opened her eyes in the garden.
"What does it look like? A river?" He said with a rather dry attempt at humour. She shook her head and the shrugged her shoulder as if she had

suddenly lost interest in knowing what the place was.

"It is a garden." He said and gently let her slide onto the slab of the fountain beside him.

She looked around again, finally talking in the beauty of the place. It was obvious that the place had been left untended for so lobby and had thus been overgrown with weed. She could see that there was no house for a stretch of space and for some reason; the whole environment seemed like the proverbial Garden of Eden. She loved it. How had he been able to find a place like this? She wondered briefly before she turned to him and decided to get on more pressing business of talking about what they had just experienced,

She opened her mouth to start talking but the look in his eyes told her that it would be better to let him unburden himself first.

He was looking into the distance as if he was remembering things that had happened in the past. Things that had happened a long time ago.

"I would have died you know... I would have died."

He started and she listened to him with rapt attention.

"She had come back and she helped me away from the place. She treated me and hoped that she would not get caught. She knew that if she was caught, she would die. Thereby was no shortcut or alternative, she would be killed."

"When I woke up and discovered that she had helped me, I knew that I had to protect her. So I went back and killed every single blood dragon that I met in the clan including the master. That way, no one would be alive to put the puzzles together. Then she showed hip in my apartment that day. The only pay she wanted was for me to give my body to her in passion. I did. She deserved it. Then I had asked her to leave because I didn't want her to be traced back to me, I sent her out into the night because I didn't want her to get clingy and start expecting much from me. I never knew I was sending her to her death."

"She texted me that night to say she was in trouble and that I should come help her out. It took me over five hours to locate her and when I did, what I found was her head and two blood dragons who had carried out the deed. Somehow, they had found out and had killed her. I killed them both in revenge but I could not bury her or give her a befitting last rite. So I left."

"She didn't deserve to die. She didn't deserve to die like that. I never wanted to drag her into this but she just would never stay away from me. I am so sorry!" His voice seamlessly ran itself over the sound of the dropping water of the fountain. It floated to her and even though she could only imagine what he must have gone through to see two women who had loved him, two women who had meant something to him, die just like that. She knew it must hurt. There really was no difference between the man and the average human male. If everyone had the power to avenge themselves and their loved ones, most would not hesitate to do it., he was just a cheated and bereaved man who happened to be trained in combat. He was doing the normal thing to do in those circumstances. He was doing what she would have done. She put a hand on his thigh and said in a low but clear voice..."

"I'm so sorry"

He nodded. It wasn't particularly comforting, he was still hurt. But he had other pressing issues at the moment.

"How do you feel now?" He asked as he ran a hand through her hair.

"Better." She said with a nod.

"Good ..." He replied as he stood up from the slab and helped her down too.

"Let's go home." He said and started to lead her towards the car. She followed him silently and dutifully got into the car when he opened the door for her. He got into the driver's side and drove back towards that apartment that she had left for over two days now.

She took the stairs in twos so that she would be angle to keep up with him as he walked. He walked past his door and towards her own. At the door, she looked into his eyes and somehow found the courage that she had tried to summon ever since the first time she laid her eyes on him. She stood on tiptoe and sliding her fingers around his head, she pulled his head down towards her face and placed a kiss on his lips. It was meant to be tentative and brief but he caught her lower lip between his teeth and keeping his head bowed at that level, allowed his mouth to stay on hers for longer than she had thought he would allow.

His tongue snuck out and teased her lips apart. Not that he had to pressure her, but he particularly loved that he had to probe around her mouth. There was something about her kiss that told him that he had better not leave without finishing what she had just started. Her mouth opened for him, allowing him to explore it like a person on an excursion. His tongue travelled around all the corners of her mouth. Teasing the corners and allowing the juice of her saliva mix with his. The kiss was deepening and the tension was mounting. This was no matter for the hallway and he expressed that by lifting her clean off the floor. Her legs wrapped around his waist and he pushed her door open. He crashed into the room and into the bed with her still in his arms. He landed on his elbow and continued the kiss without leaning into her or letting his weight fall on her.

He lifted his body from hers and removed the last of his shirt in one clean move. He then pulled the shirt that he had used to cover her body. It was a gentle pull and she didn't resist him. She laid there in the glory of her beauty.

He leaned in and kissed her passionately. Letting his mouth trail down her neck slowly. He was leaving a burning trail of desire everywhere his lips touched. She arched her back and pushed herself towards him. His hand came up and cupped the beautiful firm mounds of her breast. He squeezed just a little and then started to tease her nipples. She moaned softly. He removed his hand from her at the first moan and replaced it with his mouth. His hand now free, trailed round her body while her arms came around his neck in a bid to keep him. Her pulse was racing and her heartbeat could be heard in her own ears. She knew that she was ready, but he didn't seem to be quite ready for her yet.

Letting actions speak louder than words, she leaned her long haired head in down towards his member. Showing boldness already as she opened her mouth wide in order to slip his thick crown inside. Letting her tongue slide across the head, she kept her hands stroking away for good measure to keep him moaning as she conducted the swirling motion. Glancing up, she pushed her mouth down further onto him, causing herself to groan as she adjusted to this fat rod. Pressing her soft lips around the shaft, she narrowed her eyes in determination. She raised her mouth back upward towards the tip, before pushing back down in a smooth and steady motion that made them both groan out. He disengaged himself and decided to return the favour.

He pushed her legs apart and let himself slide down her body. His tongue found its way to where she was wet and warm and seemingly ready, his lips closed around her pulsating clit with a sweet soft vengeance. His mouth was exploring her, licking and sucking and pulling simultaneously.

He started to pull it but without applying too much force. He let go off it after a while and tasted her juice. It tasted like strawberry for some reason to him. He felt her arch her back and with a strong tongue licked her from her vagina opening upwards. He stopped and started to suck on a small bump just above the opening. The girl started to shiver with ecstasy when he started sucking on her clit. Her legs threw themselves far apart, giving him maximum access to her moist delight.

His tongue dived into her and that was when he encountered it. In disbelief, he tried again and encountered the same hurdle of flesh. Still not believing what he thought he was feeling, he started to slip a finger in. That was when she jerked and he realized that his suspicion was true.

He rose himself away from her.

"Are you kidding me right now?" He asked and she shook her head.

"Nope ... I'm not kidding you." She said with a small smile. He started to motive away from her instantly but her hand clamped around him and pulled him closer.

"Please..." She said with a voice that was pleading and burning with desire at the same time. He hesitated and shook his head gently.

"But..."

"Please...!" It was a choked plea. "I'll probably hate myself later" he said and kissed her nipples again. She drew his head to her while he kissed away and let his hand massage her clitoris. Then suddenly, he turned her over such that they switched positions. She was now on top of him with her legs hanging on each side of him. He put his hands out and grabbed her waist. Gently, he lowered her over him like he would slide a Katana into a sheath. She adjusted to him till he got to the barrier.

"This might hurt." He warned her and before she got the chance to ruminate non it, he pulled her over him. It was gentle but firm and the barrier caved without much ado. The pain was sharp and she would have screamed not she had had more time to get her breath. He waited for a few moments and then started to move gently. Slowly at first. But she started to move faster than him. Demanding and pressurizing him to go faster. Unable to keep up with her, he switched their positions again and this time let her stay below. Using his elbows as support, he allowed his waist to start the journey of pleasuring her. Kissing her as he slid in and out of her with a fervency that built a volcano in her cervix. Her moans of pleasure resonated around the room and bounced off the walls as she wrapped her legs around him and pushed him in deeper and deeper. She was too tight, contracting against him and pushing him over the edge. He could feel this tension gathering all over this body and as he approached the hill and increased his pace, she seemed to instinctively know and increase her pace too. They count to each other and moaned in incision. Their bodies intertwining and following a beat that only the two of them could hear.

The harder he moved, the more she moaned and

begged. He could feel himself ready to explode and began to push faster and harder and told her to take her fingers and rub her clit – he wanted them to come together. She did as he told her and touched herself and felt so fucking incredible. She had no control, she was going to come and she whispered to him that she was ready.

With timbres sounding in both their heads, they reached the peak of their passion and released themselves.

When it was done, he collapsed against her and remained in her arms till they both slipped away into the comforting oblivion of sleep.

Chapter 11

A smile was playing around her lips. The lazy smile of a woman who had just gotten thoroughly satisfied, forget the fact that it had been hours since she climaxed like a woman who had been having sex since forever, she was still feeling the shivers of the thorough orgasm in her spine and the thought of it was making her excited. She turned in her sleep, her eyes were closed her hair was rumpled. She didn't need to open her eyes to know that she looked a mess. Something was missing... she frowned slightly.

Something was missing. Something that had been in the room before but was now saliently absent. She started to turn in her sleep again and suddenly knew what it was that was missing. A man had been on her chest earlier but now he was no longer there. *"He must have gotten up for fear of weighing me down with his weight!"* she thought to herself and smiled again. She stretched her hand across the bed and tried to find him but the other side of the bed was empty. Empty and cold. No one had been there for hours.

She lurched out of bed as if she had been stung by a bee. Her eyes were open and she was suddenly wide awake. She looked around the room, trying to figure out where he might be. She got out of bed and walked towards the bathroom with a smile.

"Hey... up so early?" she called as she flung the bathroom door wide open. It was empty. She looked all around the place but there was no trace of him. In fact, she really couldn't prove that he had been there at all. She was starting to go crazy when she saw the note on the other pillow in the bed. She opened it and instantly, her eyes started to fill up with tears.

"Amie... if you are reading this then I am probably already far away.

You are such a wonderful girl and I am so lucky to have come to know you here. But as you have found out yourself, being with me will just constantly put you in danger. I can't let anything happen to you because of me. Women have died for my sake and I cannot have you join them too. The truth is that they will not stop coming after me. For as long as I am around you, you will be in danger and I cannot bear it at all. I am so sorry but I have to leave now. I want you to know that I love you so much and it is my wish that sometime in the future, we will meet again. I will miss you peeping at me through that hole in our wall... I will miss you looking out for me. I can't run away from my past anymore and I have to face it. Until I have this problem of the clan solved permanently, I will not come back to look for you. I love you so much, stay safe my peep hole girl. Goodbye."

Amie threw the note to the bed and rushed out of the room wearing only her pyjamas. She was crying as she ran through the street to look for him from one corner to the other. She went into the coffee shop which still remained unoccupied and derelict and looked all around the place for him but he was gone. When it became clear to her that she would not find him in those streets, she returned to the apartment. Crying profusely even though she could not even summon enough strength to make a sound. The tears just continued to fall without restraint.

"Why... why... why!" she cried inside her over and over again. When she got into the apartment, she looked around the place and it suddenly started to feel empty and lonely. Even though he had not been there for too long he had left his imprint all over the bed and all over her body too. The bed remained rumpled and the sheets remained blood stained. Evidence of the way she had given herself up to him in totality of her body and soul the other day. She fell into the bed and cried her eyes out as she suddenly realized that he was right. If she wanted to stay alive, she would need to be away from him and not he associated with him in any way. He needed to get himself sorted out before he could make any permanent emotional connections.

She knew it.

He knew it.

It was the part where she had to accept it that remained difficult and heartbreaking. She shivered over and over again and curled up in her bed. Refusing to leave the confines of the room for another four hours. When she eventually gathered herself together, she had quietly started to pack her stuff back into her pink luggage. She needed to get out of that town before it took away her sanity for good.

When she was done, she looked up and looked to the left and noticed that the window blinds were pulled apart. She walked over to the window and looked outside. Below was a busy street with streetlights going all the way to the vanishing point of her view? She stood there, watching the cars go up and down the street with a smile on her face. He had left the blinds open so that she would see the street below. The sun was rising from that part of the house and she was watching it emerge gracefully from behind the clouds. How did he know that she had never parted the curtains? How did he know that she had never experienced the beauty of the rising sun? The way the sun seemed so close to where she was, as if she could reach out and pluck it out of the sky. She remained standing by the window for a while, drinking in the beauty of the rising sun.

She would miss him, she knew that bit. There was no argument about it. Somehow, even though their time together had been short, she had been able to come to know him intimately. She was amazed that he had known all the while that she had been watching him through the hole in the wall and not only had he not minded, he had acted like he didn't know just so that she wouldn't stop. He had not blocked the hole and had made a point of giving her the best views possible. How much did the guy know? She wondered. Did he also know that she had been masturbating over and over again while watching him dress, undress, sleep, eat, and practically do anything? Did he know that she had fantasized so much about the night they had just spent together? Did he know that her lust for him had gradually transformed into a hot blistering love that burnt within her very soul? Did he know that she often had dreams about him? How much did he know?

She wanted to cry some more but she knew there would be no point. So she picked up her phone instead and called her mother. The phone had barely started to ring when she picked up.

“Hey darling! You finally remembered that you have a mother. What is wrong with you? You have had me worried sick and I was this close to booking a flight and coming down there. Why do you like to put me through this sort of stress girl? You really should stop... I will not have it. If you make me come over there, I don’t care if you are an adult, I will bundle you all the way back home. I let you go for five seconds and this is what you do to your old mother?” her mother was raving on the phone and Amie listened with lover in her heart and tears in her voice. If only the woman knew how close she had come to losing her only daughter. If only she had known how close she had come to having to identify her body by looking at her decapitated head. How was she to tell her, other that she had been this close to being rapped and brutally murdered? How was she going to tell her mother that she had been abducted by Japanese gang members and that she had slept with one who was so crazy or loyal to the clan that he had gutted his best friend just to show loyalty? How was he to tell her mother that for all of the warning she had received about joining the wrong crowd, she had somehow managed to fall in love with a man who killed eight men in about fifteen minutes. She closed her eyes and rested her head back, taking in the voice of her mother as some sort of balm to the mental and emotional bruises she had sustained in the course of her stay in this small town. Who would have thought that she would find the trouble she had spent all of her life avoiding in a small British town?

"Amie... Amie... are you there? Are you going to say something?"

"Mom..." she muttered but as much as she tried to keep her voice level, it broke and when the word "mom" came out, it was laden with all the feelings that she had been feeling for a while now.

"Amie? What happened? Hey... hey girl what is it? Are you okay? Are you okay? Do you need me to come over there? Baby are you sick?" her mother was going off and she almost started to laugh at the thought of her mother actually knowing what had gone down with her.

"Mom... calm down already... calm down. I'm okay. I just have a headache." She had made up her mind that there was no point telling her mother. How was she to tell her mother that the Japanese people that had been put on TV had mostly been killed in front of her?

"I don't think you have a headache babe. I think there is something bothering you. Did a boy break your heart?"

"Mom I'm not fifteen anymore!"

"I take it a boy broke your heart then. If that is the issue, don't worry baby... you have just two months now and you are going to be done. I am looking forward to welcoming you home."

She was silent for a moment. Her mother was right. A boy had broken her heart. Well... she had always known that her mother knew her well enough. She had been her only confidant since her father died and even now that she had not actually told her what was happening, she still managed to make a good guess.

"Mom... "

"Hmmm?"

"I miss you so much" her voice was breaking again. He mother was silent for a moment

"Are you sure you are okay baby? I could take the next available flight you know..."

"I'm okay mom... I'm just a little emotional today."

"I miss you too Amie." Her mother sighed into the phone.

"It's so empty in here without you." Amie thought and cleared her throat.

"I'll call you later... got to go."

"Don't take too long to call again baby!" her mother called over the phone.

"I won't." Amie said into the phone with tears in her voice again. Then she hung up quickly before her mother would be able to say something.

"I will" she said to herself as she walked back out to grab a bite.

Chapter 12

Her experience in the little town of Colerain had left an indelible mark on her. It had been years since she had been there last. In fact, it had been six years since she had left the town and at first, she had subconsciously waited for her heart throb to show up again. She would sit by the window and look out into the street. Waiting, praying that for some reason he would get it into his head that she was in danger again and would come rushing to her.

She had developed a habit of visiting the coffee shop, waiting for Amanda to reopen but it did not happen. She was confused. Where was Amanda and why was the coffee shop still not working. It had been months since the fights in the coffee shop, she ought to have bounced back by now. If anyone, her regular customers would have continued to patronise the place. Amie would walk through the place, hoping to see a sign that someone was cleaning the place out and trying to get the place working again but nothing had happened. The place remained abandoned and Amie remains silently confused as to where Amanda could be. She had stopped coming for her rent and after two months had passed without Amanda showing up, she had decided to ask around.

One hot afternoon, she had walked over to the coffee shop again and had seen an old homeless looking man in front of the place. She had moved closer to him.

"Hi... she had said to the man but he had not responded. She had brought out some money out of her purse and handed it over to the man. He had smiled at her with his coloured teeth and looked into her eyes.

“Hey... I know you. You are the girl who lives in Amanda’s apartment!” he said and Amie could have leapt for joy at the happiness that flooded through her at that point.

“Yes... I am. I was going to ask you if you have seen Amanda. Do you know where she is?” she had asked the old man and he had shaken his head in sadness.

“She is at the home. She got shot here by some hoodlums you see. The bullet went in her head and messed her up in there. Now she cannot talk or recognise people anymore!”

Amie stood there. Shocked out of her wits. Her mind had worked furiously because she remembered clearly the last time she had seen Amanda. She had been on the floor but not because she had been shot and definitely not in the head she had been breathing. She knew this because she had seen the woman’s gigantic bosoms rise and fall and she had not had any blood on her. Amanda had not been shot in the fight that day. She had been shot after. Someone had gone back and shot the old woman. Sadie had broken down in tears. She had thanked the old homeless man after getting the address of the "home" where Amanda was being kept. She had taken a cab over there and had sat with the older woman for three hours. Ever since that day, Amie had made it a point to send a check of at least two hundred dollars to the home for the upkeep of the wry old woman who had been nice to her.

She had thought over and over again, wondering why anyone would have gone back to hurt an old woman whose only offence was in being in her own coffee shop at that time if the day. Why would anyone try to kill her? Amie was sad, but she was glad that Amanda was at least alive.

"I'll make sure that she is taken care of." She had said to her and had stood by that promise even though it had been six years since she had last seen the town. She had made sure that she called the town once a month to confirm receipt of her cheque and to ask about Amanda's health and general well being.

Was that enough? Maybe not. Considering the fact that she felt that she was partly responsible for Amanda getting shot. She wanted to go visit. She wanted to see her every once in awhile but her life was fast changing. She had her mother to look after and she had her dog Terry to take care of. Perhaps most importantly, she had her job and her patients. The responsibility was great and she would not be having the extra time to travel halfway across the world just to see one person.

She pushed a pencil into her mouth and frowned guiltily. Amanda was not just a person... she was...

"Dr Lancaster... you are needed in OR 4...Dr Lancaster... please report to OR 4" she jerked out of her thoughts. She was still not used to the name "Dr" it felt strange to her even though it had been over four months since she had been inducted into the midst of orthopaedic surgeons. She was not used to it. Not in the least.

Her mother had been so proud of her. It had all

been a dream come true and it had seemed to her that things couldn't actually be better. She was a woman that had seen a lot, experienced so much and suffered so much. She had had to struggle to keep them afloat because the law had executed her husband's hundred thousand dollars life insurance and estate to the last letter. They had only supplied feeding allowance and education fees for mother and child respectively. Every other thing, they had had to work for. For a while, Amie had felt some resentment towards her father for placing everything on such a condition. Why would he make her graduation from college the only criterion for her to get her due? She had thought it mean and insensitive but as time passed and she realized what she had made of herself after she became a certified medical doctor, she realized that this was what he saw. This was what he had envisaged when he made college mandatory as the only way she was going to get her hands on the money that he had saved up for her. He had made sure that she would have something to fall back on should she ever become broke. He had made sure that she would never have to be dependent and this was the biggest gift a man could give his children, she knew now that she appreciated him. She knew now that she no longer resented him and in the place of the resentment was a love and adoration that could never be quelled. Now she was not only making her mother proud, she was making herself proud with everything that she did and every move that she made in life.

Dr Amie Lancaster got out of her chair and headed for OR 4. She was walking so fast that she did not see the hospital mail man that approached her. She bumped into him and banged her head on his lips.

"Oh lord... I'm so sorry. So sorry" she said to him. The mail man held his jaw in pain and made a rather failed attempt to smile.

"Here... this is for you." He said to her and handed her an envelope. She took it and stuck it into her ward coat and continued to rush towards the operating room as she rubbed her forehead.

"Lord please... when will ever stop being such a

clumsy person?" She asked herself as she pushed the door to OR4 open and slid into the place.

"Could you change please... we have an emergency surgery!" her senior supervisor doctor said to her.

"Yes sir..." she answered back with an instant readiness to work.

She dragged herself through the hallway and into the hospital car park. It had been a long night and she was glad to be free finally. She was not eligible for a break or vacation yet, but she had convinced her colleague to take her shift in the coming week with a promise to take her own shift later. She had decided that she needed the rest especially after all the mental stress she had been experiencing lately. She needed to find a balance between her present life and the life she had known before it. One would think the years in medical school would have prepared her for life as a doctor but it hadn't. At least not fully. As she would find, the stress of being a doctor was so immense that she felt overwhelmed in the first few months. She had quickly come to understand that the workload would not reduce and there would always be someone who had broken a femur or a scapula. There would always be someone whose hip bone had been shifted or broken. It was just the bitter truth of life.

She released herself into her car heavily. As she started to throw her ward coat to the backseat, she noticed that there was something that felt like paper in it. She pulled back the coat and dipped her hand into the pocket of the coat and felt around it. It was an envelope. She suddenly remembered that she had gotten the letter from the hospital mail man. She took the envelope out of her coat and tore it open at the edge. The letter fell out and fell open to her palm. She didn't need to read to know who it was from. The minute she saw the handwriting in the note, her heart started to pound so fast that she had to drop the note and hold on to her chest for a minute. She took a quick glance around in fear that he might be somewhere in the vicinity. When she didn't see him, she relaxed a little bit and picked up the sheet of paper that had fallen out of the envelope. She looked at the handwriting on it again and sighed. It was him quite alright.

"*Meet me in the old apartment peep girl!*" it said. The message was simple and the scrawl was clear. There was no argument about it. It was him alright. She looked at the back of the envelope, hoping to see the return address but there was nothing on it in that regard. She was staring at it for minutes. The memories of how she had pinned for him over and over washed over her. The thoughts of the days she was lost and couldn't study and the nights that she had been unable to sleep. She had found a sudden distaste for masturbation in her mind and over and over again when she tried to pleasure herself, she would find it almost impossible to attain any amount of pleasure through it as her mind would continue to go to him. She had endured the frustration of dates and meetings that would chiefly involve her sitting and staring at the person all through the time they would spend together. She would then respond to all their questions with monosyllables. She would then conclude that they were uninteresting and idiotic at the end of the date and never take their call again. Her mother had noticed the cycle and had gotten so worried that she might never find a man. She had come into her room one night and had asked her point blankly.

"What happened in Britain, Amie" She had asked and Amie had looked up at her with a feigned surprise. She had started to say something but her mother had held a finger up in the air.

"If you are going to lie to me then don't say anything Amie. But just know that as your mother, I am worried about you and I want the best for you. I won't be here forever and I don't want you to be alone. If there is something you need to tell me, then you better tell me soon." Amie had been silent after that and had looked away from her mother instead of looking her in the eyes and lying to her. Her mother had nodded and had looked away from her. Tears were in her eyes too and it was obvious that she was trying valiantly not to break down in tears. Amie wondered if she should just tell the woman the truth and move on from it.

"*But it has been such a long time and I have since*

moved on from it!" she had then said to herself and decided against talking to herself about her experience in Colerain. Now as she stared at the piece of paper that she held in her hand, she knew that she had not moved on from Colerain at all. She was stuck on the place so much that she had never actually bothered to move her things out of her old room totally. She had been paying someone to maintain the house and now she had just received the note to meet there by the one man in the world who knew of her history with the place. She closed her eyes and rested her head on the headrest of the car seat. She was taking deep breaths and waiting for the surge of emotions that had welled inside her to subside. Who did he think he was? Leaving her like that and disappearing for years at a stretch. Why was he asking for a meet now? Had he finally resolved his issue with the blood dragons or was he finally ready to put her life at risk if it would mean that she would be with him for as long as they were both alive? What was the aim of his not exactly? He had known where to send the note so he knew what sort of life she was living now. How could he suddenly expect her to leave her job and her patients and come looking for him in Coleraine? What if she had not just made the arrangement to have her colleague take over from her? What if she had not planned a vacation before? She was angry, but she was delighted at the same time. She was glad that even though it had taken him the whole of six years, he had finally been able to come back to her. She shook her head in surrender to the feeling of love that was suddenly welling inside of her and picked up her phone.

"*This is bell airline how may I help you?*" The lady on the other side of the line said.

"Yea... I'll like to book a plane ticket to Colerain Britain please..."

"*Sure ma'am... what are your details?*"

And that was it. It was decided. She was going halfway around the world again. This time around, she was not going to be studying in the little town; she was going to be meeting the man she loved.

Epilogue

She stood in the middle of the room, looking around as if she was scared that she would get kidnapped all over again. It had been 4 years but the room seemed exactly the same as she had left it that morning in July. It was neat, it was tidy and it still had the hole in the wall. She smiled a small mischievous smile to herself as she stood in front of the peep hole and stared at it for minutes. She could remember the day she had put her chair near the wall and had watched over him till she slept off and had a nightmare. She could remember how she had watched him through the wall, having sex with that hot Japanese woman who had wound up dead. She could remember everything and it started to seem like her whole life in that room was starting to play in front of her eyes. There was no question about it, she had missed the house. She had missed the feeling she had gotten from it and now that she stood in it again, she wondered if she would want to leave again.

She moved closer towards the peephole and looked

at it. It was as if she was metal and there was some sort of magnet on the other side that was pulling her closer to the wall. She bent towards the wall and put her eye over the wall. What she saw was the same thing she had seen that day.

That very first day.

He was naked from waist up and was standing facing the hole. The minute she put her eye over it, their eyes met in a romance of recognition. She jerked away from the wall and screamed. She rushed out of her room and headed down towards his room. She pushed the door open as if she had every intention of yanking it off its hinges and rushed at him like a lion towards a deer. She lunged at him and landed squarely in his arms with her legs wrapped around his waist.

"OH my god! Oh my god!" she was screaming and he was laughing and they were hugging each other tightly like their lives depended on it. She would kiss him, pull back and the rush at him all over again. They were kissing and she was crying. His hair was much longer now, almost reaching the middle of his back. She ran her hand through his hair and planted wet kissed all over his face. He responded in full dose and held her close while she alternated between crying and laughing. She held his face away from his and said through her tears.

"We are not cats yet?" he nodded and laughed. He held her close and let himself fall into the bed.

"Are you here to stay?" she asked him. He nodded into her hair and her tears increased.

"We are better like this, Amie... I did the right thing..."

"Yes... you did. But I'm not sure I'll ever forgive you" she grumbled. He laughed and buried his face in her neck.

"I love you." He said

"Show me" she said.

And he did.

The end.

Conclusion

Thank you again for buying Hidden!

I hope you enjoyed reading it as much as I enjoyed writing it.

Thank you so much and until next time!

Author's Bio

Lyanna Thomson is a passionate and rebel romance writer, born in Georgia. She is one of the only few writers who loves to take on action romances, with exciting badass badboys and strong willed heroines. Her stories are filled with breathtaking tension, a pinch of sexiness and full of raw emotion and passion between her characters.

Reviews matter...

If you enjoyed my book, please think of leaving a review on amazon. It would mean the world to me and will help with providing you with another book with as much emotion and raw passion as this one.

Thank you!

Preview of next book:

Chased

A spy romance story

What happens when Maria, an unusual town girl, falls for a secret spy who is being chased by his former organization?

Now in production.

CPSIA information can be obtained
at www.ICGtesting.com
Printed in the USA
BVHW071104181019
561475BV00001B/165/P

9 781607 967491